PAGALPANTHY

...IF YOU LOVED SOMEONE

MRITYUNJAY KUMAR MISHRA

Made with ♥ on the Notion Press Platform
www.notionpress.com

To you.
Yes, **you—the one holding this book.**
Since this is my very first novel, I couldn't think of anyone more deserving.
This one is for you, my reader.
Thank you for giving my words a home.

Contents

Contents

Contents

Foreword

Pagalpanthy is not just a story—it's a confession, a longing, and a mirror for anyone who has ever loved someone a little too deeply, a little too recklessly, and perhaps, a little too late. Within these pages lies a world where silence speaks louder than words, glances carry the weight of years, and love refuses to follow logic.

This is a novel born from the friction of memory and imagination. It walks the blurry line between what happened and what should have, between truth and emotion, between the heart's chaos and the mind's helplessness. Mrityunjay Kumar Mishra, in his debut, doesn't offer polished answers or idealized love stories. Instead, he gives us raw moments—awkward, tender, bitter, beautiful—and invites us to sit with them.

At its core, Pagalpanthy is about the courage it takes to remember and the madness it takes to move on. **It is a reminder that love, in its truest form, is not perfect. It falters, it hurts, it heals. But it never really leaves.**

So, if you've ever waited for a message that never came, loved someone who couldn't love you back in the same way, or whispered stories to the void just to feel heard—this book is for you.

Read it slowly. Feel it deeply. And if you find yourself between the lines, know that you're not alone.

— **Pagalpanthy**

Preface

When I first began writing **Pagalpanthy**, I didn't know I was writing a novel. I was simply trying to make sense of a time in my life that refused to stay silent—a time filled with unsent messages, unspoken truths, and a love that never quite fit into the boxes people like to label.

Someone told this story ten years ago. It stayed with me—half-told, half-felt—and I began putting it into words, unfinished and unsure. I later shared this half-written story with my friend and business partner, **Jordan Akins**, who believed in it more than I did. He kept urging me to finish what I had started, to give the silence an ending.

But like most emotional things, it lay untouched for years. And then came May 15, 2025—something happened that cracked open an old silence and turned it back into words. *I don't know if it was fate, memory, or madness*. But it brought me back to the page, and this time, I didn't stop until the last word was written.

This story is fictional, but it carries the weight of many real emotions. It is stitched together from moments I witnessed, stories I lived beside, and feelings that outgrew the confines of memory. It is about the beauty and brutality of first connections, about the tangled bond between affection and responsibility, and about the kind of love that lingers long after goodbye.

Pagalpanthy is not a love story in the traditional sense. It is a journey through confusion, chaos, and contradiction—the very things that often accompany our deepest human connections. *It is about two people, deeply flawed and deeply drawn to each other, trying to find meaning in moments that never quite made sense.*

If you've ever fallen in love when you weren't supposed to, or held on when the world told you to let go, this book may echo something familiar. If nothing else, I hope it reminds you that your emotions are valid, your memories matter, and sometimes, madness is just another word for love.

Thank you for picking up this book. You're about to step into a story where logic takes a back seat, and the heart drives—even when the road disappears.

— **Mrityunjay Kumar Mishra**

Acknowledgements

My Parents
Every bit of credit begins and ends with you. From teaching me how to read to shaping how I think, your early lessons became the foundation of everything I am today. No amount of gratitude could ever match your sacrifices. This book breathes because of you.

Rityunjay
To my younger brother—your quiet presence has been a source of strength through every chapter of my life. Thank you for standing by me, always.

Bibha, Sudha, and Soni
My dear sisters—your unwavering belief, heartfelt encouragement, and endless laughter have lit my path. Thank you for lifting me up, always.

Jordan Akins
You were the first to see something in this half-written story—and the one who refused to let me abandon it. Just like in our business ventures, you pushed, reminded, and reignited the flame. Your belief never faded, and your support never faltered. This book found its ending because you never let me forget its beginning.

Sumit
You've been more than a friend—more like the brother destiny forgot to assign. Your ideas, your presence, and your timely words have carried me through rough waters. Thank you for being there—steadfast, real, and irreplaceable.

To Everyone Else
Whether you knew it or not, your words, your silence, or your presence helped shape this journey. For every small nudge, every kind glance, and every moment of belief—thank you.

Prologue

Pagalpanthy – If You Had Loved Someone

Some stories aren't written to impress.

They're written because someone, somewhere, couldn't breathe until they were told.

This is one of those stories.

It's not about perfect love.

It's not about grand gestures or cinematic endings.

It's about two souls who met when they weren't ready, held on when they shouldn't have, and let go when it hurt the most.

It's about that one person who entered your life like a whisper and left like a storm.

The one who made your heart beat louder, your days brighter, and your nights unbearable.

This book is not fiction.

But it's not entirely real either.

It's a memory. A longing. A madness.

A **Pagalpanthy.**

If you've ever stayed awake just to see someone's last seen,

If you've ever typed and deleted a message a hundred times,

If you've ever waited for a reply that never came—

Then maybe, this story is yours too.

Thank you for opening these pages.

I hope you find a piece of yourself between the lines.

And if nothing else—

I hope you remember that even unspoken love has a right to exist.

Note: About ten years ago, someone I knew shared this story with me. It left a mark—and inspired what you're about to read.

With all my heart,
Mrityunjay Kumar Mishra

CHAPTER ONE

LAST SEEN

I still spend half my nights — sometimes all of them — scrolling through your profile, staring at your photos like they hold answers I missed the first hundred times. My heart won't listen to reason. It keeps insisting, That's her. That's the one you loved. That's the one you lost. But you're not her anymore. And maybe, I'm not me either.

Your smile in those pictures still disarms me. It shouldn't — not after everything. But my heart doesn't forget so easily. It remembers the girl who once laughed at my dumb jokes, who whispered secrets in the dark, who said she couldn't imagine life without me.

I remember everything.
And you?
You've moved on. Silently. Effortlessly.

I visit your WhatsApp, pretending I'm just "checking," but I know what I'm doing. I stare at that word —Online below your name
Then last seen at 2:13 AM.
And just like clockwork, he goes offline around the same time. The same guy you used to lie to me about — "He's just a friend," you'd say, your eyes avoiding mine. Now he's the one who keeps you awake through the night.

Do you even realize how many pieces of me you broke?

We don't talk anymore. I still can't believe it. From spending hours on the phone, sharing stories, secrets, silences... to this void. This excruciating silence.

Sometimes, I dial your number — not to call, just to stare at it, hoping maybe you'll feel it across the universe. That invisible thread. That tug. That longing.

I miss you.
God, I miss you.

And the worst part?

You don't miss me at all.

You don't want me back.

I keep telling myself I need to move on, that forgetting you is the only way forward. But how do you forget someone who became part of your soul? Is it even possible?

The nights are the hardest. That's when your memories return like a tide — relentless, merciless. I remember the way you said my name when you were sleepy. I remember how your voice cracked when you laughed too hard. I remember the songs you loved, the way you hummed off-key without caring. I remember us.

But now, I'm just a stranger who once knew you too well.

You stopped replying. You stopped explaining. You just vanished into this new life, and I was left behind with unanswered messages and questions that echo in my chest like gunshots.

I cry sometimes. Not out loud. Quietly. The kind of crying that leaves you hollow. The kind that you feel in your bones.

I remember you once said, "One day, you'll leave me when you get tired." You were wrong.

You got tired.

You left.

And I'm still here — watching you be online for someone else, pouring your laughter into someone else's midnight, loving someone who isn't me.

And that bastard — him — the one who replaced me so easily... I hate him. I hate how he gets to see you smile. I hate that he holds the version of you I once called mine.

I've tried to hate you too. God knows I've tried. But my stupid heart? It still takes your side.

I'm drowning in memories. I can't think. I can't breathe. My mind is a battlefield of 'what ifs' and 'what went wrongs.'

I don't know how to stop loving you.

I don't even know if I want to.

Sometimes I pray for a miracle — that you'll message, that you'll call, that you'll say "I miss you too."

But the truth is, even miracles seem to have given up on me.

And on nights like this, I wonder...

If I screamed into the void loud enough, would you hear me?

Would you care?

Because I'm still here.
Still lost in you.
Still yours... in a world where you're no longer mine.

Just a few days ago.
Her message blinked on WhatsApp:
"I'm not angry with you. I just want to say... I loved you, and I'll miss you. But I'm sorry — I can't be with you anymore. Goodbye... take care."
I stared at the screen for minutes before replying, my hands trembling, my mind already spiraling.
"Okay... please go. I won't stop you. I promise I'll never come back into your life again. I'll delete your number — and I expect you to do the same.
But before you leave, at least tell me why. What did I do wrong? Is it because of Avi? Are you leaving me for him and just looking for an excuse?"
Her reply was instant. Cold.
"Stop blaming Avi for every stupid thing you do. Avi was never important to me. God, why am I even explaining myself to you again? Bye."
Me: "Bye..."
And just like that, it ended.
No closure. No answers. Just silence.
I broke down.
Cried like a child who had his favorite toy — no, his only toy — snatched away by someone bigger, someone stronger, someone who didn't care.
I tried to find reasons to hate her. Any reason.
I begged my mind to give me something — some flaw, some betrayal, something that would make it easier to let go.
But nothing worked.
Even the worst things she did weren't enough to poison the love still pulsing in my chest.
So I cried. Not like a man, but like a boy — heartbroken and helpless, knowing that what was once mine was gone forever... and there was no hope of getting it back.

CHAPTER TWO

THE FIRST PING

It was December. Cold, quiet — the kind of month that makes you reflect.

Back then, I was just a guy with a dream. A big one. I wanted to become a business tycoon, the founder of a globally recognized tech firm — someone who would be remembered not just for success, but for building something from nothing.

That dream began the day I unwillingly stepped into the world of engineering — my so-called "punishment" — choosing Computer Science not out of passion, but pressure.

I wasn't the kind of student parents brag about. I never had top ranks, never topped boards. Wasted time, laziness, and a lack of direction made exams like IIT-JEE and AIEEE slip through my fingers. But somehow — maybe by a stroke of luck or a rare error in copy-checking — I landed a decent rank in Odisha JEE and secured admission into a reputed private college.

That's where things began to change.

Somewhere between assignments, late-night coding, and caffeine-fueled deadlines, I discovered something that actually lit a spark in me — programming. For the first time, something felt right. It wasn't a burden. It was a calling.

And with that, I made a decision: I wouldn't settle for a job after graduation. I would build something of my own. I'd carve a space in the software industry as an entrepreneur.

Fate — or maybe something more poetic — brought me together with two classmates who shared the same fire. We weren't just students; we were co-dreamers. That's how "UniSys Solutions" was born — our small software firm with big dreams.

We poured everything into it — days, nights, heart, mind, sleep, and soul. We weren't earning much. In fact, most months we barely broke even. But we were learning. Growing. Evolving. And somehow, that was enough.

Guiding us through it all was Dr. Vinay Patra — our professor, our mentor, our anchor. He believed in us before we believed in ourselves. It was because of him that we had a space to work — a decent setup for a ridiculously low rent, all because he wanted us to chase our potential.

During one of our software engineering lectures, I remember hearing something that stuck with me: "There's no shortage of software companies. But there's always a shortage of good developers — the ones who innovate." That line became our mission.

We weren't just building software. We were building ourselves.

It was December of 2013.

Bhubaneswar wasn't exactly cold — it never really is — but the weather had that rare, comforting touch. Crisp enough to feel pleasant, soft enough to make you smile without a reason.

I was working, as usual. It was around 11 a.m. on the 22nd, a Sunday. That day is still etched in my memory — not because anything remarkable happened right away, but because something small began.

Out of sheer habit — one of my worst at the time — I opened Facebook while taking a break. Notifications, friend requests, pointless scrolling... the usual. Among them was a new request from a girl. Nothing new — I often received requests from classmates, school friends, or people I'd met through events.

But this one was different.

I didn't know her.

No mutual memories. No shared conversations.

Curious, I checked our mutual friends. That's when it clicked — she was probably the daughter of Dr. Vinay Patra, our mentor, our guide, and the man who made our startup dreams slightly more real.

I found it odd. I'd never seen her, never even heard her name. All I knew was what Dr. Patra had mentioned once or twice — that his daughter was in 12th grade and preparing for her boards.

Still, I accepted.

The next day, I noticed her online. Something nudged me to text her. Maybe it was curiosity. Maybe fate. Or maybe it was just boredom wrapped in digital courage.

Me: Hi!
Her: Hi :)
Me: Are you Dr. Patra's daughter?
Her: Hmm.
Me: How do you know about me?
Her: It's not my fault ☺ *Papa always mentions you when I ask him anything technical. He says, "Ask him, he'll help."*
Me: Ohh... I see :)
Me: Had lunch?
Her: Nope. Mumma's still cooking.
Me: Why don't you go help her out?
Her: Hehehe... tried once. Almost blew up the kitchen :D
Me: Hahaha! At least learn to make Maggi — that'll save you in hostel life.
Her: Ohho! So you also think I'll make it to IIT? :D
Me: Why not? Just focus a little — you'll crack it easily.
Her: I've lost interest in studies... even the board exams feel like a mountain.
Me: So what's the backup plan?
Her: I'll drive an auto-rickshaw.
Me: Brilliant! Apply for a license soon — and tell your dad to buy you a shiny new one :P
Her: Hehehehe
Me: Will you charge me if I book your auto someday?
Her: Never! Free rides for you :D
Her: By the way, IITs are chasing me hard... I can't decide which one to join!
Me: I know. I was the one who recommended you.
Her: Oh really? What did you say?
Me: They were looking for an auto driver... so I suggested your name :D
Her: :D Usually I pull people's legs... but today, you got me!
Me: Hahahaha!
Her: Okay bye!
And just like that, she went offline.
I smiled. And replied:
Me: Bye...

CHAPTER THREE

THE FIRST GLIMPSE

December 25, 2013

Christmas morning. No snowfall in Bhubaneswar, of course, but the air still carried a kind of festive stillness. For most, it was just another winter day. For me, it would become unforgettable.

I opened Facebook late that morning, as usual, and found my inbox flooded with messages. All from one person.

Soumya: hi..

Soumya: hello..

Soumya: :o :o :o

Soumya: der?

Soumya: ;(;(;(;(

Soumya: pls reply :(

Soumya: :o :o :o

The sheer number of emojis made me smile. None of my friends were fond of smileys — I wasn't either, until I read somewhere that Indians statistically use fewer emojis than people in other countries. Since then, I'd made a conscious effort to throw in a few here and there.

But this girl... Soumya? She was a champion emoji user.

Me: Hi

Soumya: Finally, you came :)

Me: Yes :) Anything special?

Soumya: I was getting bored. Do you have any good movies? I want to spend my day watching something.

Me: I have a hard disk full of them. You can take it. But why not study? Your board exams are just around the corner, aren't they?

Soumya: I'll study later. First, I'm coming to get your hard disk, if you're not using it.

That made me pause. Until then, we hadn't met face-to-face, despite the fact that she lived just next door — in a duplex adjoining our small workplace. I was nervous. Not because I had anything to hide, but because she was Dr. Patra's daughter. Our mentor. What would he think if he found out that I wasn't just chatting with his daughter on Facebook, but also lending her movies?

Me: Is it okay for you to come here like this?
Soumya: Why wouldn't it be? What's the big deal?
Me: Hmm... okay. But please let your mom know.
Soumya: Done :)

Two minutes later, the doorbell rang.

I opened the door to what felt like slow motion.

She stood there in a purple top and black jeans, hair loose and curly—clearly uncombed, but effortlessly natural. She wasn't wearing any makeup. She didn't need to. Her curls tumbled over her shoulders in defiance of any comb. No filters, no pretenses—just the quiet confidence of someone who didn't care to impress anyone.My eyes dropped before they could betray me. My tongue turned dry. I forgot how to say even 'hello.'

And oddly enough, not once had she used her real photo as a display picture. This—this unguarded, unfiltered moment—was the first time I truly saw her.

I couldn't meet her gaze. Not directly.

I handed her the hard disk, muttered a polite "Here you go," and she thanked me with a quick smile before walking away.

A few minutes later, she pinged again.

Soumya: Hello :)
Me: Hi
Soumya: Would you mind if we stopped being so formal and just talked like friends?

I paused for a second. Formal?
Was that what this had been?
Were all those smileys... formal?

Me: Sure. Why not?
Soumya: Actually, I wanted to ask — can you lend me your headphones for a few hours? Mumma is sleeping and won't like loud sound while I watch the movie.
Me: Okay. Come and get them.

My heart felt warm all of a sudden — excited, alive. Not because of headphones, but because I'd get to see her again. I tried hard to hide my joy behind a neutral face when she rang the bell. I handed her the headphones as casually as I could.

She promised to return them in a few hours.

Exactly two hours later, she was back — returning both the hard disk and the headphones.

Me: Which movie did you watch?

Soumya: You really have a great collection. I've been looking for a film called "The Vow" for ages — since the day it was released. Finally found it in your hard disk!

She smiled and left.

Her words kept echoing in my head.

The Vow. What was so special about that movie?

Without a second thought, I opened my laptop and started watching it. It was a romantic drama — a heart-touching one, filled with love, memory, and longing. I liked it. Not just the film, but the idea that she liked it.

In that moment, I realized something simple and obvious:

She was like every other girl I'd never dared to get close to.

She liked love stories. And unknowingly, she had already become one in mine.

CHAPTER FOUR

THE SPARK

December 28, 2013

The days were crawling by, and our startup dream was being kept alive not just by ambition, but by stubborn hope. We were three — Hitesh, Dhiraj, and I — chasing something we couldn't yet touch: our own product, our own place in the world of software. But dreams don't pay electricity bills or buy groceries.

Hitesh was still employed at a reputed MNC, but Dhiraj and I had quit our jobs — against the will of our families, against conventional wisdom, and perhaps, against better judgment. There was no financial backup, no monthly salary cushion. Just a few aging laptops, an unreliable internet connection, and an intense belief that something would eventually click.

To make ends meet, I had started bidding for freelance projects online. Mostly on sites like Freelancer.com. But as newcomers with no reviews or credibility, we were practically invisible. Each bid felt like shouting into the void.

Still, that day — December 28 — something changed.

I submitted yet another proposal, just like I'd done a hundred times before. But this time, a message popped up in our inbox.

A client from overseas had responded.

He asked a few technical questions, and we replied with trembling fingers and a lump in our throats. Minutes later, we were awarded the project.

It wasn't a big one — just a few hundred dollars for building a small search feature, something similar to what eBay used. But to us, it felt like winning the lottery. Our first international client. It felt unreal.

We jumped, we shouted, we hugged each other like children. Hitesh, even after his full day at work, stayed up all night with us, working on the project with unmatched energy. That night, our little room — barely big enough to hold our desks — was filled with the quiet hum of ambition and the louder roar of hope.

For the first time in weeks, I forgot about Facebook. I forgot about chats. I forgot about her.

January 1, 2014

The project was going strong, and so were we — sleepless but driven. It was New Year's Day, but for us, it was just another workday. We had decided not to waste the first day of the year in the usual way. No pointless resolutions, no lazy mornings. Just work. Maybe something special for lunch.

Hitesh suggested we cook something memorable. I agreed.

Around noon, the doorbell rang. It was Dr. Patra's mother. She'd come, like always, with a small tray of sweets. A kind gesture we had grown to love.

But that day, I had a different idea.

"Why not celebrate together?" I offered. "Let's make lunch — proper lunch — and eat it as a family."

She smiled, pleased. We decided on poori, shahi paneer, and a sweet dish. Something simple but festive.

By 2 PM, the food was ready. I called her down.

Fifteen minutes later, the door creaked open.

And then I saw her.

Soumya.

Not in a casual tee and jeans. Not with uncombed hair or quick smiley replies. Today, she appeared in a saree, and she looked... unreal. Like she'd walked out of a poem.

Every poet struggles to capture beauty in words. But what I saw that day — no couplet, no canvas, no song could do justice to it. She wasn't just beautiful. She was grace. A soft, divine kind of beauty that made my chest tighten. She looked like the brushstroke of a master painter. Radiant, serene, and somehow distant — as if the world had paused just to let her exist in that moment.

Her eyes had a quiet power in them. Her smile wasn't there yet, but her presence said everything.

I felt something electric — not love, maybe not even infatuation. But something had changed in me. A spark. The kind that sets dry hearts on fire.

She entered with her grandmother and parents. I welcomed them with all the composure I could gather, though my knees felt strange and my heart was racing.

We all sat for lunch together.

And during the entire meal... we didn't exchange a single word.

I kept avoiding her gaze — not out of disinterest, but out of nervous awe. She was no longer the girl who once joked about pulling rickshaws or borrowed headphones from me. She was someone else now. Or maybe, I was seeing her differently for the first time.

When they left after lunch, I stood in silence.

There were so many things I wanted to say.

But the only words echoing inside me were:

"You look like a dream."

CHAPTER FIVE

SUCCESS AND SILENCE

Six relentless days. Countless hours. Almost no sleep.

That's what it took to complete our **first international project** — a simple search engine module, yet a milestone for three young dreamers trying to carve their place in the software world.

After endless coding and repeated testing, we were finally ready to submit. But instead of claiming "job done", we played it smart — we told the client, "Please check if everything works as expected." It was safer that way. If there were bugs, we could still pretend the work was "in progress."

The client, Mr. D'Costa, happened to be online. As we waited, the tension in our small workspace was so thick, even the blinking cursor on the screen felt like a heartbeat.

Then — ping.

"Excellent job," he wrote. **"This is exactly what I was looking for."**

It was 4:00 AM. We were physically exhausted, but those two words recharged us like electricity to a dying bulb. Moments later, the **$250** milestone was released — our first earnings from a foreign client. Fifteen thousand rupees in hand, a 5-star rating, glowing feedback — we'd made it, even if it was just the beginning.

It wasn't just money. It was validation. Now we had credibility. Now, future clients might notice us. Now, maybe, we could breathe a little while chasing our bigger dream.

Without thinking twice, I logged into Facebook — maybe just to tell someone who'd been on my mind despite all the hustle.

Me: "I'm extremely happy. We've successfully completed and delivered our first overseas project. Got a 5-star rating too. Bye and good night."

That was it. A small message to Soumya. I didn't expect much. Maybe just a smiley. A "congrats." Something.

I turned off the lights and lay down, tired but content.

The Next Day

Saying it out loud felt surreal.

"Our first international project."

We shared the news with Dr. Patra. He was genuinely pleased. His encouragement always meant something more than mere politeness.

But strangely... no reply from Soumya.

She hadn't even seen the message.

I stayed online most of the day, hoping to catch a glimpse of her name. Nothing.

By evening, the mystery solved itself — while chatting with Dr. Patra, I learned that Soumya had moved to her hostel. Apparently, he didn't believe she could focus while studying at home.

It puzzled me. Why let her stay here for so long, just to send her to a hostel weeks before exams?

I didn't ask more. But a subtle sense of disappointment settled over me. She wasn't just missing from Facebook — she was missing from my orbit.

Still, the evening brought new energy — we won another project from a Canadian client. This time, it was a dynamic blog redesign. Sleek UI, clean code. We were excited. This wasn't just freelancing anymore — it was momentum.

A Few Weeks Later

We had just delivered our ninth project. Business was rolling. Projects were stacking. We were coding day and night. For three ordinary guys, things were starting to feel... extraordinary.

But success brings fatigue too. And that day, I felt like I deserved a break.

"Let's take today off," I told Hitesh. **"No clients. No code. No brain games. Just masti."**

He smiled. "Same plan here."

I logged into Facebook, almost out of habit. It had been ten whole days.

And there she was.

Soumya — online.

Was she back from the hostel? Maybe home for study leave?

Either way, it felt good to see her name again. Without hesitation, I messaged:

Me: "Hiii!!!"

And then... nothing.

Ten minutes passed.
Then twenty.
At the thirty-minute mark, her chat showed "Seen."
She was still online. But not a single word in response.

It stung more than I expected.

It felt like saying hello to someone face-to-face... and they look you in the eye, then just walk away. Not a word. Just silence.

I logged out without saying anything further.
That evening, Hitesh and I stepped out to eat something — anything to distract from the strange ache I felt.

Was I angry? Not really.
Was I hurt? Maybe a little.

But more than anything, I was confused.
And somewhere in the middle of that confusion, I realized something unspoken was changing.

CHAPTER SIX

The Gift, The Goal, and The Girl

January 22, 2014

A date etched in my memory — the deadline for our own ambitious creation. Not a client project this time, but our innovation. A special kind of search engine — not for websites or files, but for physical items inside malls and big shops.

The idea was revolutionary. We called the hardware component **Location Mapper**, a device that mapped the entire mall into identifiable zones, each marked with a unique location ID. Products, tagged with cheap chips similar to RFID stickers, constantly reported their location to a central server. Users could then search for items using a local web portal, just like using Google — but for finding lost socks, scattered toys, or a pair of headphones dumped in aisle seven.

Throw anything anywhere — our system could find it. That was our USP.

It worked flawlessly in our little lab — a cramped 300 sq ft room — but scaling it required funds. So we turned to the one hope that fuels all dreamers — venture capitalists.

VCs were everywhere these days, and honestly, getting a pitch appointment felt easier than ordering a pizza from McDonald's. We submitted our proposal and waited, hoping for that golden call.

Meanwhile, we couldn't ignore client work. Survival money still mattered. Among our most reliable clients were Leon Koh from Singapore — young, smart, and constantly sending us freelance projects via WhatsApp — and Shiv Aiyer, an NRI from Kerala now settled in Dubai.

Shivam ran **AMR Freight**, a logistics company with branches in 12 countries. He wanted us to build a centralized inventory management system. It was a massive project, and when I quoted $20,000 , he didn't blink. He even offered to fly us to Dubai for on-ground research — all expenses paid. He'd be in Bangalore in April to finalize things and would help with our visa too.

When I ended the call, Hitesh and I were practically bouncing off walls. It felt like winning the FIFA World Cup — for India — without ever kicking a ball. The deal wasn't even finalized yet, but the hope alone was intoxicating.

And there was one person I had to share it with — **Soumya.**

I logged into Facebook.

To my surprise, she was online. My heart jumped. I'd messaged her earlier, but she hadn't responded. I asked about it.

She said the messages weren't delivering because she was chatting with old friends. A contradiction so obvious it made me chuckle — messages weren't working only for me, apparently. But I said nothing. Maybe I didn't want to ruin the moment.

Instead, I poured everything out — the Dubai offer, the project, the excitement. And her reaction?

She wanted to come see me right away.

Fifteen minutes later, there was a knock at the door. And there she stood, smiling, holding... a bitter gourd.

A karaila.

I blinked.

She laughed. "I wanted to give you something. This is all I found."

I took it, laughing too. My first gift from her — a vegetable. I joked, "You should've cooked it before gifting."

She replied with one word, playful and soft:

"Paglu."

And just like that, she gave that silly word a kind of weight I'd never imagined.

I don't know if it was the word or the girl — but that moment stayed with me. Still does.

Later, she asked me to join her on Facebook again.

Online Chat

She: Hi!!!

Me: Hi ☺ First tell me — when did you come back? Weren't you at the hostel for studies?

She: Umm... I came back yesterday. I don't want to study. I left the hostel.

Me: What?! You're giving boards in just 1.5 months and you left hostel?

Why? What's bothering you?
She: I'm just done with it. Tired. I want to do something big, something different. But not study.
Me: But to do anything big, you need knowledge. You have to study.
She: You don't know what I've gone through...

And then she opened up — about eve-teasing, harassment, and feeling helpless. She'd even written an article and shared it with her warden, who dismissed it with a line:
"Focus on studies. Stop thinking rubbish."

That cut deep — both for her and, strangely, for me too.
She wanted to help other girls. To change the system. To do something real.

And I wanted to help her — starting with something basic: getting her to study again.

Me: Let me help. Just for a few days. Trust me. Give it one honest try. Please.
She: If you can do that, it'll mean a lot. I promise I'll do whatever you say.

We decided to start small. I'd take her online test the next day. IIT-level questions, just to see where she stood.

That evening, after a quick lunch, I sat down and carefully crafted her first test. 30 questions — 10 each from Physics, Chemistry, and Math. I pulled from old IIT papers, solved each one myself in case she needed help later, and uploaded it to my own local examination portal.

It took me 4 hours. But I didn't mind. For some reason, it felt... worth it.
At 5:00 PM, I logged into Facebook.
Me: Hello.
She: Hiii
Me: Studied anything?
She: Yes! Electrostatics and a bit of math.
Me: Great! The test questions are pretty standard, so you'll need to focus.
She: I'll try my best, I promise.
Me: Books or notes?
She: Notes — they're faster to finish.
Me: Smart choice. You've got 24 hours left.
She: I'm not sure how well I'll do, but I'll give it my best.
Me: Good. Now log out and study.
(I didn't want her to. But I wanted her to succeed more.)
She: Okay. Bye!
Me: Bye.

That night, I felt a mix of anticipation and something I couldn't name. Maybe it was purpose. Maybe it was hope. Or maybe it was just the way she said Paglu — like I mattered in a way I hadn't realized before.

23rd January, 2014 – Facebook

When I logged into Facebook...

Soumya: Arrey... I was waiting for you. I need to talk.

Me: Yes, tell me.

Soumya: I studied dipoles and electrostatics!

Me: Nice.

Soumya: Now I can't do anything more. Thanks so much for your support. But your efforts are useless... I just can't do this. Please leave me.

Me: Why are you so frustrated? I see you online every time I log in to Facebook. How will you manage to study like this? You're wasting too much time here.

Soumya: No, I'm not. No one trusts me. But I swear, I had just logged in now. There's no point explaining it to you—I know you won't believe me.

Me: Look, I do trust you. Don't get so frustrated. There are just 30 objective questions—just attempt them. Based on what you've studied, you'll at least get an idea of where you stand. Don't worry, I won't post the result anywhere, and I won't be angry either. Trust me.

I was 8 years older than her and had some idea of how to handle someone emotionally overwhelmed. Thankfully, it worked. She agreed to take the test.

Me: Go to this link and register for the test: https:///register*

Soumya: Okay... what do I put in the password field? My Gmail password? ☹

Me: No, silly! Enter any password—you just need to remember it.

Soumya: Okay... done!

Me: Now log in and start the test. All the best!

Soumya: Okay, but please stay online... don't go anywhere.

Me: I'm right here. Don't worry ☺

Soumya: Thanks...

Ten minutes later...

Soumya: So much time wasted. Oh God... My standard is so poor. I didn't even submit the test—it auto-submitted and I scored 0%! ?

Me: What? Let me check. Did you refresh the page or open another tab?
Soumya: Yes, I refreshed it...
Me: Okay. I'm resetting the test. Attempt it again, but don't refresh or open any other tab this time. And no cheating! ? Meanwhile, while I reset it... you can go ahead and cry for a bit if you want ?
Soumya: Muuuuuuuuummmmmmmmmmmaaaaaaaaaaaaaaa!! ??
Me: Start now! All the best!
After 2 minutes...
Soumya: Cheating!! You changed all the questions!
Me: Nope! Look carefully—only the order has changed, not the questions
?

Soumya: Ohhh yeah... ? Sorry. Now don't disturb me. Let me concentrate!
Me: Great! Keep an eye on the timer too!
Thirty minutes later...
Soumya: I've messed everything up. It's all over. I scored just 18% ?
Me: Don't worry. Nothing's over. In fact, it's good that you scored 18%—and that's without proper preparation. We can work together to raise that to 80+%. This test was just to show you where you stand right now. You still have a full month left, and a good strategy can work wonders!
Soumya: I know you're trying hard. But honestly, I don't care about anything anymore. I just want to escape from all this. You won't understand!
Me: Why do you think I won't understand? Talk to me... trust me... maybe I can help you.
Soumya: Just help me change my mood. I want to do anything other than study. I don't even want to appear in my board exams. I've been behaving weirdly with everyone. I've lost my peace. I just want to be happy again. I want to come out of this darkness.
Me: Okay, forget the board exams for now. First, tell me—why are you feeling this way? Why are you so hopeless?
Soumya: Because I'm a loser. A big one. And I don't want to waste your time. I don't even know why I'm behaving like this. I don't want to do anything... especially not study. There was a time when studying was my top priority. I was a topper. But now? My only priority is peace of mind. And I feel helpless. Whenever I see a pen, I feel like stabbing myself with it. My brain just doesn't work anymore.
Me: First of all, you're not wasting my time. And second—you're too young to be called a loser, you silly girl. I know something's bothering you deeply. You can talk to me, anytime. For now, I have something else to teach

you—something fun, not academic! And trust me, you're not helpless. I'm here for you. Just trust me, and listen to me. Everything will be okay—better than ever.

Soumya: Really? I hope so. What fun thing will you teach me?

Me: Go eat your lunch. I'll eat too. We'll talk in 30 minutes. Deal?

Soumya: Okay! But don't forget. I'll wait. And if things really get better, I promise I'll study. No one will need to force me. Just trust me.

Me: I trust you. For sure.

I had three pending projects—one of which was due for delivery that very day. But still, she was my priority. I didn't know what kind of magic she was weaving just by being herself, but something was definitely there. I was sure—she was going through depression. She was mentally exhausted, hopeless, and broken.

And I had made up my mind: no matter what, I would help her get through this. I'd make her happy again, and help her do well in her exams too. I had that confidence in myself.

Strangely, I was happy too. I didn't know why—but every interaction with her made something in me feel alive. Even with deadlines looming and pressure mounting, things felt... lighter.I caught myself humming while typing code, her last message still glowing in another tab like a quiet presence.

My team noticed the change. Hitesh laughed, *"**Boss, startup chal raha hai ya love story likh rahe ho?**"*

It was something magical.

CHAPTER SEVEN

After lunch, I logged in. She was already online. Her profile picture had changed, and her cover photo now had some inspiring quote.

She: "How's my profile pic?"
Me: "It's good. And nice quote."
She: ☺
Me: "So, are you free?"
She: ???
Me: "Why are you showing your teeth?"
She: "Because you're asking if I'm free ?. I have lots of time... sooo much!"
Me: "Okay! Then first of all, tell me—do you have any idea about the language used to build websites?"
She: "HTML!"
Me: "Great! So, do you know what HTML stands for? And are you interested in web designing?"
She: "I'm interested in learning anything that's not part of my course... HTML stands for Hyper Text Markup Language."
Me: "Genius! How do you know all this?"
She: "It was part of my +2 syllabus. They taught just a little bit."
Me: "Do you want to learn web designing?"
She: "Gladly! But only if you have time..."
Me: "Pagal! I always have time to teach. I love teaching!"
(In reality, many juniors used to ask me to teach HTML, Java, etc., but I was often too busy. But for her, teaching felt pleasant—like a joy.)
She: "Then okay!"
Me: "Now, show me what you really know. Design a simple webpage and write 'Soumya is an idiot' using all six header tags. You have 10 minutes. Clear?"
She: "Yes, clear! Wait, I'm doing it..."
Me: "Good. All the best."
She: "What comes first, head or title?"

Me: "I don't know... you just do it first. I'll correct it later if needed."

She: "Hmm... okay!"

Me: "Now start! Good luck."

    8 minutes later:

She: "Hi!"

Me: "Yes... done?"

She: "Not sure if it's right or wrong. But it's working."

Me: "Send it to me—attach the page and send it via message."

She: "Okay."

    She sent me an HTML file. When I opened it in the browser, it showed:

    Soumya is Cute!

(repeated six times using different headers)

    Me: "Good work. But there are some serious errors!"

She: "I knew it... please tell me the errors."

Me: "Well... the first error is: you wrote 'Soumya is cute', which is not true. ?"

She: "Haaaawww ?"

She: "Bye... hate you!"

Me: "Arrey, listen! Actually, the correct sentence is 'Soumya is the cutest.'"

She: "Awwww... really?"

Me: "Yes ☺ "

She: "Then okay!"

Me: "☺ But there are other errors too. See, the <head> and <title> are misplaced. Here's the corrected version—check the attachments."

I sent her the corrected file. We spent two hours, and to my surprise, she was a great student—quick to learn, genuinely interested.

I promised her a Dairy Milk for her effort.

She learned almost all HTML basics that day. I promised to teach her CSS the next day so she could design her own website. She was happy and said it was the first time in a while that she had done something meaningful. She thanked me.

But honestly, I wanted to thank her—because teaching her gave me a feeling I couldn't put into words. It was amazing.

Before logging out, I told her to revise everything and create something new. She agreed happily.

I delivered one of three pending projects that night and went to bed at 4:00 AM. I woke up around 10:00 AM and, as usual, logged in.

She was already online. My chat box was flooded with her messages:

She: "Hi!!"
She: "There?"
She: ???
She: "Still sleeping? Get up, please... been waiting for 2 hours!"
She: "Wake up—it's too late!"
She: "Arrey, finally you're here! You sleep so much!!"
Me: "Slept at 4 AM last night. Had a project to deliver."
She: "Ohh, sorry. You promised to teach me CSS today."
Me: "Yes, I will. But give me 30 minutes to freshen up. You also have breakfast, okay?"
She: "Okay! See you in 30 mins. Bye."
Me: "Bye."

I got ready and came back online within 30 minutes. She was already there—probably waiting!

Me: "Hi."
She: "Hiiiiii ☺ "
Me: "So, are you ready?"
She: "Yes ☺ But let's chat a little first."
Me: "Great idea!"

She told me she had shown her dad the HTML page she made. He was very happy and encouraged her to learn more. He also said, "Mrinal is good at programming—take his help whenever needed." I felt good.

Then she joked that she told her dad I call her an idiot and sometimes harass her.

Me: "Whatttt??? Do you know what I want to do right now?"
She: "Yes—you want to kill me ?"
Me: "No, I want to beat you with a broom—idiot!"
She: "Really? Okay wait... I'm coming!"

After two minutes, she rang my doorbell. When I opened the door, she was standing there—smiling, no, laughing—with a broom in her hand! She offered me the broom and pretended like I should use it.

She looked so cute and innocent that I just laughed. I took the broom and said, "I'm not a fool to beat you with this lightweight broom. I'll kill you!" and laughed again. She joined in.

That silly moment brought us even closer. It was one of the best memories so far.

Me: "Since you're already here with a broom, why not clean my room too?"

She: "Hey Bhagwaan, utha le mujhe. I have no respect left!"
Me: "Okay, okay, stop the drama. Let's start CSS now."
She: "Yes, okay."
On Facebook:
She: "How was that?"
Me: "You're an idiot—but the cutest idiot. And a big one!"
She: "Hehehehehe... I knew that! Say something new ☺ "
Me: "Okay, let's start."

I taught her how to style web pages—change colors, use divs, etc. She was brilliant—quick to learn and full of curiosity.

After two hours, she could make a decent-looking web page.

Me: "Now I'll give you a task: create a three-page website—Home, About Us, and Contact. Here's the design on paper—replicate it in HTML/CSS."

She was very happy and thanked me a million times. I could feel that she was improving. She had stopped talking about suicide. I felt proud because I was the reason.

I had started working late nights so I could be free to talk to her during the day. I found myself thinking about her all the time—even smiling at her silly actions and the cute little things she did.

It wasn't love. Not from my side. She was 8 years younger. But I definitely liked her company—badly. I even enjoyed talking about her with friends. Life had become colorful, even though I knew all this was temporary.

But I wanted to live every moment.

February 9, 2014

She: "I'm going back to the hostel ☹ Tell me honestly—what's better, studying at home or in the hostel?"

Me: "Why are you going? Definitely, the hostel is better for studies... but I want you to stay here at home."

She: "I have no choice. Papa is sending me ☹"

Me: "☹ Then go, and study hard. Remember, you have to score more than 85%! If you do, I'll give you a surprise gift."

She: "Really?! But in the current situation, I think I can only pass... So not such a big expectation. But I'll try."

Me: "Good. All the best! When will you be back? After the exams, I guess?"

She: "Yes, no chance before that."

I was feeling weak. I didn't want her to go. But it was about her studies—and she had to go. Still, I asked her to meet me once before leaving. I wanted to give her something. Something that might keep her happy. I was worried that at the hostel, she might slip back into that depressive state.

I still didn't know the exact reason behind her depression, but I was trying my best to pull her out of it. That's why I wished she could study here at home.

She came in the evening.

She was wearing a purple top and black pajamas. She looked sad—but still, damn cute.

I asked her softly, "So... you're really going?"

She leaned her face and replied in a low voice, "Yes."

I could feel her sadness. Maybe she liked home more than hostel. Or maybe it was something else. But I just wanted to see her smile. So, I joked:

"Pagal! You're not going to your sasural (in-laws) that you're this sad. Cheer up! You'll be back after exams anyway. And if you ever feel low there, just call me anytime, okay?"

She: "Phones aren't allowed in the hostel..."

Me: "Hmm... Still, you can borrow one from someone if needed, right?"

She: "Yes."

Me: "I have something for you."

She: "What?"

I had a black Pierre Cardin pen—lucky for me, and something I really loved. But I didn't have anything better to give her. So, I handed it to her as a gift and wished her all the best.

She was feeling low. And so was I.

Despite the 8-year age gap, we were talking like close friends. I knew I was going to miss her—badly.

I asked her to write a few lines about me in my diary and sign it. I wanted something from her—something I could hold on to whenever I missed her.

She said she'd take the diary to her room and write there, then return it. I said okay. She left with it.

An hour later, she returned.

She gave me the diary and said she was leaving right now. Then, with a smile and a gentle warning, said: "Open the diary only after I've left, okay?"

I nodded.

The moment she left, I opened the diary.

On the last page, written in beautiful handwriting, with both smileys—happy and sad—she had written:

"Although I don't exactly know what work you do, I know one thing—you have to be at the top in your field.

Mujh jaisi nikammi ladki ko bina bore hue itna zyada help karne aur itna sab kuch sikhane ke liye, jitna bhi thanks bolu, kam hai...

(No matter how much I say thank you, it will never be enough for helping a useless girl like me so much, without ever getting bored, and for teaching me so many things...)

You don't know, but honestly, I needed someone to support me mentally—and that is what you did! That was the real help. Many many thanks for that! ☺

I know I'm going to miss you badly ☹ *But I hope we'll meet very soon.*

I have a small suggestion for you too: Please take some rest, okay! ☺

Love you,

Soumya Patra

(Signature)"

I didn't know exactly what she meant by "Love you."

Girls sometimes say things that confuse guys. Maybe it was just affection. Or maybe more. I couldn't tell.

But whatever it meant—it made me feel awesome.

I read that message again and again. Her words made me smile every time.

Whenever I missed her (which was often), I opened the diary, wrote my feelings, and read that last page. It became a routine—to read her words at least 10 times a day.

I also started keeping my Facebook tab open all the time, checking every 10 minutes—hoping she'd come online.

I used to message her updates—what project we got, from which client, and so on. But there were no replies. She wasn't logging in.

I even wished her exams would get postponed, so she could come home.

But that was just me, living in my hopes.

Was she thinking about me, too?

THE SPACES BETWEEN US

Everything was going great.

Our work was flourishing day by day. We had finally taken an office space in the city—with enough capacity to house 30 team members. We took a bank loan of ₹10 lakhs to furnish the office and purchase the required equipment.

For the three of us—Dhiraj, Hitesh, and me—we built individual rooms, decorating them just the way we wanted. It truly felt like we were living our dream.

We soon began recruiting people to join us. Some private engineering colleges even invited us for campus placements. But we chose to visit coaching institutes like NIIT instead. Personally, I believed they taught exactly what the corporate world needed—practical, skill-focused knowledge.

This was our first ever recruitment drive. We were going to conduct interviews for our own dream company.

Our office was freshly set up, decorated, and ready to welcome candidates. All three of us—excited, nervous, proud—were prepared to sit on the other side of the table.

There were 200 applicants for the job, but we needed just 30, including two experienced candidates.

We designed a 3-stage hiring process: a Written Test, followed by a Technical Interview, and finally an HR Round.

After the written test, only 90 candidates qualified for the technical round. We divided them among the three of us and began the interviews.

The first candidate entered.

We exchanged quick smiles and wished each other luck.

Candidate: "May I come in, sir?"
Me: "Yes, please."
Candidate: "Thank you, sir."
Me: "Please take your seat."
Candidate: "Thank you, sir."
Me: "May I know your good name?"
Candidate: "Harish Mohapatra."
Hitesh: "Are you comfortable?"
Harish: "Yes, sir."
Hitesh: "Great. You've mentioned programming is your passion. That's good—we like passionate people. But you'll need to prove that."
Harish: "I'll try my best, sir."
Me: "Good. Tell me—what do you mean by caching in web development?"
Harish: "No idea, sir."
Hitesh: "Java is your area of expertise, right?"
Harish: "Yes, sir."
Hitesh: "Alright, write a small program to swap two numbers using only two variables."

It was a common interview question—almost a standard one. But unfortunately, he couldn't answer it.

Dhiraj also asked him a few more questions, but the outcome was clear. We thanked him and moved on.

It took us 5 hours to interview all 90 candidates. Out of those, we selected only 8—2 girls and 6 boys.

Yes, our expectations were high. But we wanted only the best. That meant we had to continue interviewing throughout the week.

By the end of that intense hiring phase, we finally had a team of 30 talented individuals who were now part of our company. It was time to celebrate!

In all this rush and chaos, I had almost forgotten about Soumya. I hadn't even logged into Facebook in over two weeks.

Even though we had an office in the city, my favorite place to work was still our old workspace. I was emotionally attached to that place. Every night, I would go there and work until morning.

My responsibilities had grown. I had to ensure we brought in good projects, delivered on time, and maintained high quality. Most nights, I had to stay up late, chatting with clients. Sleepless nights became my routine—but I was used to it by now.

Then came the morning of March 10.

It was around 8:30 AM. I had just fallen asleep after another long night of work.

Suddenly, my phone rang loudly.

Everyone close to me—including my partners—knew that this was my sleeping time. So, I rarely got calls then.

Groggy and surprised, I checked my phone.

It was Soumya.

Wow! My sleepy eyes instantly lit up. Just seeing her name was enough to chase away all the tiredness.

I picked up the call.

Me: "Hello! Where are you?"

She: "My exam starts in an hour. I'm very scared."

Me: "Oh no! Why scared? I know you'll do your best. It's just another exam—treat it like any other. What subject is today?"

She: "Math. Your favorite!"

Me: "All the best! And remember—whatever the result, I'm on your side. So just relax and give your best. This isn't your first exam, and it won't be your last. So why worry? I'm always here for you. Everything will be fine."

She: "Pakka sab kuch thik hoga na?" (Are you sure everything will be okay?) Her voice sounded soft...and sad.

Me: "Yes, pakka. Do you trust me?"

She: "Honestly, I trust only you."

Me: "Then go, and give your exam. I'm always with you. Okay?"

She: "Thank you. I feel so relaxed now."

Me: "All the best. Bye!"

She: "Bye."

I wanted to tell her everything—the new office, our team, our interviews, our progress.

But I didn't want to disturb her focus before the exam. So I stayed quiet.

Yet one thing she said kept echoing in my mind:

"I trust only you."

That sentence meant the world to me.

I made a silent promise:

"No matter what happens, Soumya—I will never break your trust. Not ever."

That one call—just two minutes long—changed my entire day.

Suddenly, everything felt brighter. I smiled the whole day.
Everyone I met noticed it—I was glowing.
Was this what they call magic?
Or was I just being stupid?
I didn't know.
But I knew one thing for sure—
I was happy.

CHAPTER NINE

FAIRYTALES, FOREHEADS, AND GOODBYES

My new office was running beautifully.

There were lots of projects, endless work, and an overwhelming sense of achievement. Life was smooth—almost too smooth. We were also progressing steadily on our dream project, which we expected to complete by June. It was March now.

As usual, after finishing up at the office, I returned to my old workplace. Even though we had a well-furnished office in the city, that old room still remained my favorite place—to think, to work, and to sleep. It held too many memories to let go of.

Just as I entered the room, I received a message on my phone.

Soumya: Hi!!!!!!!!!!!!!!!!

The moment I saw her message, I couldn't resist. I called her instantly.

Me: "Hello!"

Soumya: "Hello!"

Me: "When did you return? How were your exams?"

Soumya: "Exams were okay. I just got back today. Where are you?"

Me: "I'm right next to your house—in my old workplace."

Soumya: "Old workplace? Wait, you have a new one too?"

I smiled and began telling her everything—how we had started getting bigger projects, how we took a city office for our organization, and how things were picking up rapidly.

I asked if she could come on Facebook so I could show her some photos of the new office. She said yes.

Just that one conversation melted away all the exhaustion of the day. Her return brought a different kind of joy. I was genuinely happy.

I quickly opened my laptop and logged in to Facebook.

It was around 10 PM. Dinner was done. My only priority now was to talk to Soumya. Literally, I was mad to chat with her.

After chatting for an hour, she said she was feeling sleepy and wished me good night before going offline. It felt sudden.

Something didn't sit right.

I had a gut feeling that she was still online but had made her chat status invisible.

We shared the same Wi-Fi network, and I knew how to check which devices were currently connected. I opened the network map.

I was right.

Her device was still connected.

Did she lie to me?

If she didn't feel like chatting, she could have just said so.

Was it just me who was so eager to talk?

I felt a little hurt. But I consoled myself—maybe she had her reasons.

I tried to focus back on work but kept checking if her system was still online.

At 3:00 AM, finally, her device went offline.

I texted her on her phone:

"Good night! Sweet dreams!"

A few minutes later, I checked Facebook again.

She had messaged me.

Soumya: Haaaw??? You don't sleep??? (Sent through Messenger)

Me: "You're still awake?"

Soumya: "I just came online, saw your good night message, and thought you might be asleep... Just about to log out and saw you online!"

She lied again.

Still, I played along.

Soumya: "Can you sing a lori (lullaby) for me?" ?

Me: "Okay! Lala lala lori, doodh ki katori, doodh mein batasha... Soumya kare tamasha..."

Soumya: "Hehehehehe! I was just looking for question distribution for JEE Mains."

Me: "Hmmm... good."

Soumya: "Do you know any fairy tale? Please spell it for me!"

She was asking so sweetly, I could've told her a hundred stories right then.

Me: "But from where will I get a fairy tale now? You tell one!"

Soumya: "Get it from anywhere! I don't care—it's your problem, not mine. Mujhe bas story sunni hai!"

God, where does she hide so much cuteness? And in so many different ways!

Me: "Okay, listen. There was a Pari (fairy)... she had a son. And then that son also had a son!"

Soumya: "...And she had a magic wand too!"

Me: "Yes, but it broke."

Soumya: "How?"

Me: "It was old and fragile... it just broke ?. Okay, leave it. Now you tell me a joke."

Soumya: "I woke up today at 5 AM."

Me: "Nice joke! Tell another one!"

Soumya: "Mummmaaaa!"

Me: "Wait... that wasn't a joke?"

Soumya: "NOOOO!"

Me: "Okay, sorry ?"

Soumya: "Jao... maaf kiya."

Me: "Thank you. You're too kind." ?

Soumya: "Battery of Soumya is now low. I want to sleep in someone's lap. But my mom is half my height... she fits in my lap ?"

Me: "What happened?"

Soumya: "Today, I just need someone—not a particular person, just... someone. But everyone is asleep."

Me: "Hmmm... that's tough."

Soumya: "Should I wake up Mumma?"

Me: "Go for it. If you want to sleep in her lap, you'll have to wake her ?"

Soumya: "Aaye haye... today Mumma-Papa's room is locked from inside. What's going on? ?"

Me: "Check again ?"

Soumya: "I checked twice! It is locked!"

Me: "Naughty!" ?

Soumya: "Who? Papa?"

Me: "You figure it out." ?

Soumya: "Not fair! A young daughter like me sitting lonely at home while parents are busy romancing? This is injustice!"

Me: "Hehehe. What should they do? Kick you out just because the mood strikes?" ?

Soumya: "Haaaw! Why are you always against me? Always threatening to throw me out ?"

Me: "Okay, okay! I'm with you now. Papa is doing wrong. Happy now?"

Soumya: "Of course! I want justice!"

Me: "Then what should I do for you, madam?"

Soumya: "I'll knock loudly and shout that I want justice and Mrinal is with me!"

Me: "Don't! That'll be injustice to them! Who knows what's going on inside the room ? You'll get your own turn someday... think of your future!"

Soumya: "Let it be! I'll keep my kids with me. No injustice!"

Me: "Liar ? I'll wait and see when your time comes!"

Soumya: "I'm not lying! Why would I send my kids away if I'm romancing?"

Me: "Even when they grow up to your age?"

Soumya: "Yes! What's the problem?"

Me: "You'll spoil them early then!"

Soumya: "Hehehehe!"

Me: "Aren't you scared of me?"

Soumya: "Why should I be?"

Me: "Just asking. You talk so freely."

Soumya: "Well, it's you. Not someone else. Why should I be scared?"

Me: "Hmm... okay."

Soumya: "Absolutely okay!"

Me: "Listen to a joke now."

Soumya: "Okay."

Me: Raju was traveling on a train. The ticket inspector came and asked, "Sir, can I see your ticket?"

Raju checked his pockets, his bag, his wallet—nowhere to be found. The inspector frowned.

Raju sighed and said, "Fine, I'll buy a new one."

The inspector replied, "That's great, but where were you planning to go?"

Raju grinned. "That's exactly what I was trying to figure out!"

Hope that brought a chuckle! Let me know if you want another. ?

Soumya: Hahahahahaha! ?
Me: "It wasn't that funny!" ?
Soumya: "No, it really was!"
Me: "Okay then, it must be!"
Soumya: "Suman Shekhar truly loved me ?"
Me: "Who's that?"
Soumya: "One of my school mate. He keeps messaging me."
Me: "If you don't like him, unfriend or block him."
Soumya: "Already done that. But so many strangers message me... I don't even know them. Suman messaged 'Hi' at least 50 times!"
Me: "Block them. It's sad how girls face this kind of behavior online."
Soumya: "It's nothing. It happens everywhere. Eve-teasing is common. People comment, and we're expected to just move on."
Me: "We need to find a solution someday."
It was 3:57 AM and I still didn't feel sleepy. I could've kept chatting with her forever.
Me: "Aren't you sleepy yet? Look at the time!"
Soumya: "Oh my God! I didn't even notice. I have to sleep now."
Me: "Yes... good night, sweet dreams."
Soumya: "Okay. Going to sleep. Please send me some lovely fairy tale in my dreams."
Me: "I've run out of stock. Sleep without one tonight ?"
Soumya: "Good night, bye."
Me: "Bye."

She logged out. I did too.

But I was smiling.

I had been so tired after work. Yet just two hours of chatting with her—talking about absolutely random things—had made my night.

I was happy.

I re-read our messages three times before finally going to sleep at 5 AM.

Thank you, Soumya... for coming into my life.

The next day, everything still felt perfect—until the message came.

"Bad news! I'm going to my mama's house for 15 days ☹ I don't want to go... but Mumma is forcing me!!"

I had just reached my office around 11:37 AM. Dhiraj and Hitesh were already there. Everything looked routine until I saw that message from her.

I quickly logged into Facebook. She was online.

Me: "Why are you going? When?"
Her: "Mumma wants to visit her brother. We leave tomorrow ☹"
Me: "Where exactly?"
Her: "A small village, about 80–90 km from Brahmapur. It's a beautiful place, but I really don't want to go."
Me: "Me neither... I don't want you to go anywhere—not even a little bit."
Her: "Itna pyaar karte ho mujhe? :P"(You love me so much?)

She was teasing, but what I truly wanted to say was, Yes, I love you more than even I understand.

I couldn't imagine a day without talking to her.

Me: "I don't know what this is. But I do know—I don't want you to go."
Her: "Arrey, don't worry. I'll always stay in touch over the phone."

We chatted the whole day. I could feel it—she wasn't happy about going either.

Then she asked for something unusual.

"Can you search for the song 'Maine Tujhko Dekha Reprise – Ragini MMS 2' on YouTube?"

I'd never heard it before.

She told me she was listening to the MP3 and found it very romantic.

I was a bit busy at the time, but because she wanted me to hear it, it became the most important thing in the world.

I plugged in my headphones and messaged her, "I'm watching it on YouTube."

Her: "Tharki insaan! I told you to listen, not watch! :P"
Me: "Arrey, what tharki?"

Then I realized—yep, the video had some pretty intimate scenes.

Her: "Close your eyes and just listen to the lyrics!"
Me: "Naah... I'm watching the video too. Hehehe."
Her: "I knew it. Tharki aadmi!"

We laughed, chatted a bit more, and then she logged out.

That evening, there was a big deadline at work. I got fully immersed with the team. By the time we finished and released the project, it was 10:00 PM. The client was thrilled, and so were we.

But then I checked my phone.

30 missed calls.

All from her.

My heart sank.

How could I not have heard the phone ring even once?

How did I not check my phone for over three hours?

I immediately called her.

No answer.

Called again.

Line busy.

My "babu" was angry. I deserved it.

I messaged:

"Sorry babu, I'm really sorry. I was caught up in the project and didn't even hear the ringtone. Please talk to me."

Called again. This time, she picked up.

Me: "Sorry, sorry, sorry! Deadline day! I didn't hear the phone, I swear. Please don't hang up. Talk to me..."

Her: "Okay, okay... thik hai. I'm not angry anymore. You called me 'babu' na."

Me: "Yes, because you are my babu."

Her: "And you're my babu too... chhota sa, cuteu sa babu."

I smiled like an idiot.

Me: "Still at the office. Will reach home in 30 minutes."

Her: "Okay. I'm waiting."

Me: "Take care. And thank you."

Her: "Thank you for what?"

Me: "For not staying angry with me."

Her: "Hehehe... how can I be mad at my babu?"

Me: "Coming soon. Bye."

Her: "Bye. Take care."

I grabbed my bike, picked up some food from Dalma Restaurant at Khandagiri, and reached home by 11:15 PM.

Messaged her:

"Just give me 10 minutes. I've reached. Having dinner."

After dinner, I tried calling her again.

Busy.

Again. Busy.

Strange.

It was 11:47 PM. Who could she be talking to so late?

I tried to stay calm. Maybe a relative. Still...

If she had called me, even if I was on a call with anyone—parents, clients, friends—I would've at least sent her a message.

But she didn't.

I tried calling again. Still busy.

My heart sank a bit.

I felt something I hadn't felt before—hurt.

And then, I reminded myself:

We weren't in a relationship.

She had every right to talk to whoever she wanted, whenever she wanted.

She could ignore me if she wanted.

But that last thought made my eyes moist.

I decided I wouldn't call again.

Not until she called me first.

I logged into Facebook, but my heart wasn't in it. I was desperately waiting to talk to her. I kept staring at her chat box, just hoping to see that little green dot. It was 1:15 AM. I wanted to call her again. Just then, she came online.

Soumya: Hi

I wanted to ignore her message, maybe just to pretend I didn't care. So I read it but didn't reply for two minutes. But honestly, I couldn't hold back.

Me: Hi

Soumya: Naraz? (Angry?)

Me: No... you were too busy to even reply to me, na? ☹

Soumya: Actually, I was on a call with a close friend...

Me: Who was that?

Soumya: I need to confess something. Please don't reply until I'm done.

Me: Okay...

Soumya: I was talking to Ansh. We've known each other for three years and had been in a relationship since December 14, 2013. But over the last few days, I felt something was off. He started ignoring me for no reason—no calls, no replies. Today, he finally called. He failed in a few subjects and blamed me for it...

As she poured her heart out, I felt a storm inside me. We weren't in a relationship—there was no commitment between us—but then why did it feel like betrayal? What about all the "babu" talk? The window chats? The late-night calls?

I felt numb. Lifeless. I wasn't even interested in hearing the rest. But I had to pretend to be normal. I was older. I had to show maturity. But deep down, I was breaking. Who gave me the right to dream about her? I thought of all those beautiful moments, and I couldn't stop the tears. That's when it hit me—I was in love with her. Truly. Madly.

Was I really so weak? Did I mistake kindness for love? Did I even deserve her?

I tried to calm myself. Sometimes, it's better to be just a friend to the person you love the most.

I continued reading her messages. She told me how it all began with a missed call from Ansh, how their bond grew, how he was a B.Tech student at IIIT Hyderabad, a skilled guitarist, part of the college band. She remembered every little detail about him. It was clear—she had loved him deeply.

She went on to say that today they broke up. She couldn't take it anymore. He was blaming her for his failures, even though she had kept her distance during his exams to not disturb him. She said she was happy now—but I knew better. She was crying. I could feel it.

I called her, but she didn't pick up. She messaged saying she didn't want to talk on the phone. That confirmed it—she was crying. Even though she was trying to act normal.

I wanted to change her mood.

Me: Listen, I want to show you a magic trick! Go to this link and download TeamViewer.

Soumya: What's that?

Me: Just download and install it. It's a small software—quick download.

Soumya: Okay.

Five minutes later—

Soumya: Done.

Me: Great. Open it and tell me the ID and password from the left side.

Soumya: 248682842 / 4099

Me: Got it. Wait a minute...

I connected to her laptop using TeamViewer. Her Facebook was open. I launched Notepad on her system and typed:

"Welcome me to your lappy!"

Soumya: Arrey... bhoot??

Me: Hehehe. No, it's me! This is the magic I wanted to show you—I can control your computer now!

Soumya: Really?!

She was surprised. And for the first time that night, she seemed to forget about Ansh. That's exactly what I wanted.

I opened a drive and played a song on her system.

Soumya: I want to control your computer now. Can I?

Me: Of course!

I gave her my TeamViewer ID and password. A few seconds later, she had full control.

Soumya: Don't touch your mouse! I'm going to find your secrets!

She giggled like a kid. She opened my Facebook, browsed around.

Soumya: Hmm... no suspicious chats. You must've deleted everything before giving me access!

We both laughed.

Then she started teasing me. She messaged one of my college friends, a girl:

"jgjggjgggjkkhkkhk"

Me: Arrey, what are you doing?! Are you trying to get me killed? ☺

She laughed and did it again—this time to Hitesh.

Hitesh: What happened Mrinal? What is this?

Me: Sorry... keys got pressed accidentally.

Hitesh: Okay... good night!

Me: Bye!

I logged out of Facebook to avoid more mischief—but honestly, I loved her *badmaashi*.

It was now 3:15 AM. I opened Notepad on my own system and typed:

"What were you doing with my friends?!"

Soumya: It's called Pagalpanthi... and I love Pagalpanthi! You'll learn soon.

Me: I already did. And I loved it. Thank you for this.

Soumya: No, I should thank you. I was really upset... but now, I feel normal again.

Me: I could tell. You were broken. And I couldn't let you cry. That's why I did all this.

Soumya: Hmm...

Me: Remember the song you mentioned earlier—the one I was supposed to see at the office?

Soumya: Oh yeah! You mean... we'll watch it together now using TeamViewer?

Me: Exactly! If you want to, that is.

Soumya: Of course! Wait, I'll play it on YouTube. And hey, we can use headphones—TeamViewer lets us talk too!

Me: You didn't tell me that earlier!

She played the song and shared her screen. We both wore headphones.

"Maine khudko de diya hai tujhko... main tera, main tera..."

The song was beautiful... but the video—God, it was borderline adult. A little too intense for us.

Me (typing): Are you comfortable?

Soumya: Yes.

Me: Okay.

We finished the song in silence.

After the video, she disconnected. I logged back into Facebook, but she wasn't there. I messaged her:

"Are you okay? Come back online."

She replied shortly.

Me: What happened?

Soumya: Nothing.

Me: You're acting weird. Are you sure?

Soumya: Yeah...

Me: Look, nothing bad happened. You're mature enough to understand, right? Please, send me a smile. I want my Soumya smiling like always.

Soumya: ☺ ☺ ☺

The next morning, I woke up at 8:20 AM—much earlier than my usual time. But today was different. I wanted to be ready early so we could spend some more time together before she left. Just then, I received a message on my phone:

Soumya: Good morning, get up now!

Me: I'm already up! Good morning! Where are you? Come in 10 minutes.

Soumya: Coming.

And within ten minutes, she was at my doorstep.

She looked absolutely stunning in a short shirt with dark blue stripes and black jeans. Her face was fresh, glowing, and full of emotion. The cutest girl on earth was standing in front of me.

Soumya: Hi.

Me: Come in. You look ready already?

Soumya: Yes... Papa said we're leaving for Mama's place at 10 AM, so I got ready early.

Me: When will you be back?
Soumya: No idea. Maybe after 20 days.
Me: Please don't go...
Soumya: Don't say that, or I'll cry right here...

I looked into her eyes. The corners were already moist. And I knew mine were too. I could already feel the ache of separation creeping in.

Me: Pagal ladki, don't cry. We'll still chat over Facebook, like always. Okay?
Soumya: Yeah... but we won't be able to do all that masti and pagalpanthi from the window...
Me: Hehehe... don't worry. When you come back, we'll do double the masti!

Then, without a word, she did something completely unexpected.

She stood up, came close... and hugged me.

Her head rested on my shoulder, her arms wrapped gently around me. But something wasn't right.

She was crying.

I slowly placed my hand on the back of her head, pressing gently, whispering:

Me: Babu, don't cry...

My voice was trembling. I was struggling to keep my own tears from falling. I held her tighter, lifted her face gently, and wiped away her tears. Then, without overthinking, I leaned in and kissed her softly on the forehead.

That did the magic. She stopped crying.

We slowly released each other from the embrace. She turned to leave, but I stopped her.

Me: Wait. Sit down for a moment.

She sat.

Me: I want a promise from you.
Soumya: What kind of promise?
Me: That you won't cry for anyone or anything again. No matter what the situation is, I'll always be there for you. But you have to promise me—no more tears.
Soumya: Okay... I'll try. But you were crying too, weren't you?
Me: No, I wasn't...
Soumya: Hehehe... liar. I saw it in your eyes. I heard it in your voice.
Me: Babu...
Soumya: Hmm...?

Me: Please don't go. Tell your mom you want to stay and learn something from me.

Soumya: Not possible now. I tried convincing her already, but she didn't agree.

Me: Hug?

Soumya: That's exactly what I need right now.

We hugged again—despite the risk. We knew someone could walk in anytime. My ears were alert, trying to catch the sound of the gate or footsteps. But I didn't care. Not at that moment.

It was a long, warm, silent embrace. I could hear her heartbeat. I could smell the sweet fragrance of her freshly washed hair. I wanted that moment to freeze, to last forever. No words. Just presence.

I wanted to say something, but she softly interrupted:

Soumya: Kuchh na kaho...(Don't say anything...)

Suddenly, I sensed someone approaching. I gently pushed her away.

Soumya: What happened?

Before I could answer, her mom walked in.

I quickly picked up a notebook and pen from the table and pretended to be teaching her. She played along perfectly.

Her mom simply came in to tell her to eat something before they left. She refused to eat. After a few moments, her mom left the room.

Soumya: Thanks for everything. You don't know how much your support meant to me.

Me: Shut up, you idiot. I didn't do anything special, okay? And from today—no more formality between us.

Soumya: Hmm... okay!

Me: Wait... I have something for you.

I searched my bag, unsure of what to give her. I found a diary.

Me: Take this. Write something in it every day. If you miss me, just write whatever you're feeling. When you're back, we'll read it together.

She loved the idea.

Soumya: Only if you promise to do the same. You'll write about me when you miss me, okay?

It was a difficult promise—how could I write something for each moment I missed her? There wouldn't be a second I didn't. But still—I promised.

She left the room. And I... I felt something shift inside me. I knew now—there was something between us. Something real. Something beautiful.

A message blinked on my screen:

Soumya: Bye!

Me: Bye... take care!

And then I heard it—the sound of the car engine starting.

She was leaving.

CHAPTER TEN

Terrace Talks and Teleportation Dreams

That day, we had delivered our 100th overseas project—and in just four months! It felt like a huge achievement. The clients were happy, and so were we. We decided to celebrate.

A cake was arranged with "100 Smiles" written on it. We had a small party with our office staff—just Hitesh, Dhiraj, and me. Everyone was genuinely happy. Once the celebration wrapped up, we left the office early.

I checked my phone. It was 7:15 PM, and I noticed a message.

"Miching yew ☹"

It was her. Sent at 6:03 PM.

Without delay, I called her.

I desperately wanted to hear her sweet voice.

As soon as she picked up, her first words were,

"I don't want to talk to you."

"But why?" I asked, confused.

"I'm narazed," she said.

It was her own version of Hindi-turned-English—like "narazed" for angry, or "mazaking" for kidding. She had such a unique way with words that every conversation with her felt refreshing.

"I'm really, really sorry," I said. "I saw your message and your missed call, but I was genuinely busy. We were celebrating the 100th successful project delivery. I just wish you were here with me to celebrate."

Her voice softened, *"Wow! Congratulations! All of this is for me, right? You're working so hard and achieving so much... just for me, na?"*

She sounded so adorable when she showed possessiveness. Her cute voice, her simple words—they worked like magic.

"Who else would I be doing all this for, if not for you?" I said, meaning every word.

I wanted to add the word "sweetheart" at the end, but I held back, scared I might cross a line.

"Hehehe... Paglu!" she giggled again. And just like that—she cast her spell.

"Can we talk in 30 minutes? I'm just leaving for home. Still at the office," I requested.

"Okay, but come home safely. Bye."

"Bye."

Exactly 25 minutes later, I was home. I had already eaten at the office party, so I was free to talk to the prettiest girl on earth.

Just before I could call her, a message popped up.

"Whr r u?"

I replied, *"Reached home... was just about to call you."*

She instantly messaged,

"Listen... go to the terrace first. Then call me."

"But why the terrace? Are you on the terrace?" I asked.

"Offoo... you ask too many questions! Just go and call me from there." She replied with her usual cute bossiness.

And how could I ever say no to her?

So, I obeyed.

I called her from the terrace.

"Okay, I'm on the terrace. Now what?"

"Look up at the sky. What do you see?"

"Stars, the moon, and the sky... what are you trying to do?"

"Look at the moon. How does it look?"

"It's probably a full moon today. It looks... beautiful. Are you watching it too?"

"Yes... I'm on my terrace too."

"Wow... we're watching the moon together. That's nice."

And then she dropped a bouncer, right to the heart.

"Do you know? If a boy and a girl watch the moon together... they might fall in love."

"*Really? So that means... you and I might fall in love?*" I teased.

"*Paglu...*"

She could've answered directly. But no—she had her own cute way of driving me crazy with her innocence. I so badly wanted to tell her that I had already fallen for her a thousand times. But I didn't have the courage.

"*What 'Paglu'? We are a boy and a girl, aren't we? Hehehe...*" I nudged her.

"*Hmm... so does that mean you love me?*" she threw another bouncer.

"*No... I didn't mean that.*" I played it safe.

"*That means you hate me? Bye! I hate you too! Huss... huss...*" she said, pretending to be angry.

"*Arrey... okay, okay... fine. I love you. Happy now?*" I gave in, just to see her smile again.

"*Pagal aadmi! You're a real Paglu!*"

It's true what they say—no one can ever fully understand a girl's mind. I wanted to express my feelings, to tell her everything... but I was scared. What if she didn't feel the same? And her responses always left me more confused than before.

So, I decided to talk about other things. I told her about the 100th project. She shared stories from her mama's village. She mentioned she would be bathing in a well tomorrow since there was no bathroom there—and she was excited about it! It would be her first open bath.

We talked for more than two hours, until she had to go for dinner.

Later that night, I wrote a poem I had read somewhere, in my diary:

"*I know I'm madly in love with you, but it's impossible for me to express...*
I know you're the best, but it's impossible for me to express...
I know my day feels incomplete without you, but it's impossible for me to express...
I know you mean the world to me, but it's impossible for me to express...
You're the sunshine in my morning,
The breeze in my romantic afternoon,
The glow of the setting sun by the river,
The wish on a full moon night... you're everything to me.
You're the beat in my heart, the smile on my face,
The tears in my eyes, the dreams in my sleep...
And even though I feel lost without you...
Still, I can't express it."

I wasn't just thinking about her anymore—she had become a constant stream in my mind, flowing through my thoughts day and night. Every phone call, every chat, every shared laugh—it was affecting me deeply.

While browsing Facebook, I came across an interesting post filled with tricky questions labeled "IAS Interview Questions." Out of habit, I shared one with her:

"Tell me, in which state is the Bay of Bengal?"

She instantly called back.

"Hello?" I answered.

"You asked which state the Bay of Bengal is in? Well... it's a sea, so it's not in any single state. But technically, it's a body of water—so it should be in a liquid state!"

Her analytical thinking left me speechless. She wasn't just guessing—she was reasoning. There was no silliness in her logic. I was genuinely impressed.

"You're a genius! See? It's the effect of my company. You're starting to think like me now." I teased.

"Shut up! I'm a born genius. Accept it!" she laughed.

"I'm proud of you," I said sincerely. "Want more questions?"

"Yes! I love these kinds of puzzles."

I asked her seven more questions, and she got five right! My Soumya was smart—and curious. She told me she wanted to do something big in science—not just follow the traditional path of studies and a job.

I asked what in science she loved most.

"Teleportation," she said.

"So what do you know about it?" I asked.

"It's when someone disappears from one place and reappears somewhere else instantly. But... how is that even possible?"

We dived into a beautiful discussion.

I explained Einstein's $E=mc^2$, and how mass can be converted into energy. I asked if she believed she was made of matter. She said maybe not—she didn't feel like "just" matter.

"Well," I said, "do you have mass and volume?"

"Yes," she answered.

"Then technically, you are matter. And theoretically, with enough energy, you could be converted into energy and then back to matter. That's how teleportation might work."

"But where will we get the speed of light from?" she asked, with genuine curiosity.

"Exactly. That's why, for now, teleportation is only possible with subatomic particles."

We ended up talking the entire night. Something as geeky as teleportation felt like magic when shared with her. Nothing was boring when she was with me.

"When are your class 12 results coming?" I asked.

"On 31st May. That day is also my NISER entrance exam," she said.

"Sixteen days left. Are you studying for NISER?"

"Not really. I'm not interested in studying—but I do want to get into NISER."

"You're good at studies. And now you're becoming even better, thanks to my company! So just study a little?"

"BYE."

"What happened?"

"You always tell me to study! I don't like studying. Still, just for you, I try to study daily. But you never stop nagging!" She was really upset now.

"Sorry... I didn't mean to upset you. Anyway, it's 4:35 AM—we should sleep."

"Okay... good night. Bye."

"Bye."

CHAPTER ELEVEN

THE MORNING CALL

It was 10:30 AM. My phone rang. I hoped it was her.

But no—it was customer care. I rolled my eyes and hit the red button to reject it. Then, without a second thought, I dialed her number.

After two rings, she picked up.

"Mela babu uth gaya?"(*"Aww, did my babu wake up?"*) she said.

Her voice. That voice. Sweetest in the universe. It tickled my right ear and my heart in equal measure.

"Just woke up," I replied. *"And you? Still under the blanket?"*

"Mekko ninni aa rahi,"(*"Sleepy-sleep is coming to me."*) she mumbled sleepily.

"Do you even know the time? It's 10:30 already!"

"Give me one big hug, then I'll get up."

God. Where did she learn to be this adorably demanding?

"How can I hug you over the phone?" I asked, smiling.

"I don't know! I just want one. How you give it is your problem!"

"Come here once... then I'll give you the tightest, warmest hug ever."

"Tharki insaan," she giggled. *"Ladki dikhi nahi ki niyat kharab!"*

(*"Such a creep,"* she giggled. *"The moment you see a girl, your mind goes dirty!"*)

"Okay, enough of this drama now. Get up, have breakfast, and come online. Fast."

"Okaaaay!"

I hung up, smiling. Then I rushed to get ready for the office. As always, I was running late.

At work, trouble was waiting.

One of our old clients from Australia had filed a dispute on Freelancer. He claimed our delivery didn't meet expectations. A hot-tempered, impatient man. Dhiraj had been managing his project, but now the responsibility was mine.

I messaged him:

"Hi, I think there's been a misunderstanding. Maybe we didn't fully get your requirements. I promise we'll redo everything exactly how you want, and you won't have to pay if you're not satisfied."

He was online. The chat started.

Thirty minutes later, we had clarity. His complaints were valid, but the changes needed were minor. I promised to deliver the updated work in two days. He seemed content. The dispute was resolved.

Finally, I checked my phone. Three messages from her.

It was 1:17 PM. I logged into Facebook. She was already there.

"Sorry," I messaged. *"There was urgent work. Now I'm free. Wassup?"*

"Do you know, I took a bath today on the well! So cold and clean. Maza aa gaya."

("Do you know, I took a bath at the well today! It was so cold and clean. I loved it!")

"Mujhe maza nahi aata... I take a bath every day," I teased.

(I don't find it that exciting... I bathe every day," I teased)

"Shut up! I'm talking about an open-air bath. In the well! The water was sooo good. I looked so fair today. You'd go mad if you saw me."

"Pagal," I replied.

"Seriously! The water here is amazing. I bathed for almost two hours. And when sunlight hits my skin—you can't even imagine how I looked!"

We were so comfortable with each other. No filters. No judgment. Just pure, honest nonsense.

"Still bathing?" I asked.

"Nooo! You won't believe what I'm doing now."

"Try me."

"I'm studying."

"Good joke."

"BYE!"

"Sorry! Just kidding."

"Gande insaan!"("You perv!")

"Okay okay. But seriously, you're bathing in the open? What if guys are watching?"

"Why would they hide? It's open from all sides!"

"Exactly! Someone could take a photo. Misuse it."

"Nothing will happen. I'm not that sexy."

"Still, you know the risks. And yet you still do it?"

"Let them watch. I don't care."

"But I do. I'd kill them."

"Jealous much?"

"Me? Never."

"Liar. You are. Anyway, I was teasing you. The well has high walls. No one can see."

"Just wait till you're back. I'll tease you properly."

"Hehehehehe."

"I'll beat you. Come back soon."

"I'd love to be beaten by you."

"I miss you..."

"Awwww... babu."

"Come soon. Please."

"I will... but not sure when."

"Hmmm..."

I didn't know what we were. Friends? Lovers? Idiots? All of it, maybe.

She told me everything. Everything. And she knew all my secrets too. No one else did. But still, there was confusion.

I was pretty sure she had a boyfriend. Ansh. She tried to convince me they'd broken up. Maybe they had. But my gut said otherwise.

Sometimes, in the middle of a chat or a call, she'd suddenly vanish. No explanation. Still online, but not replying. Later, she'd blame the network or her phone.

Whatever this thing was between us, one thing was clear — when we didn't talk, even for a few hours, I felt empty. The day dragged. My focus dropped. If she didn't say "good morning," my whole rhythm broke.

I didn't care what label we had.

I just wanted to be with her.

CHAPTER TWELVE

SHADOWS BENEATH THE SMILE

It was 5:00 PM, and I was still at my desk in the office when a message popped up on my phone—one that sent a jolt through my chest.

"From today onwards, you don't need to call or message me. Bye forever."

I froze.

Staring at the screen, I re-read the words again and again, hoping I'd misunderstood. My fingers scrambled to scroll through our chat history, desperate to find where I had gone wrong. Had I said something? Missed something?

Panic took over. I called her. No response. Called again. Still nothing.

I messaged:

"What did I do? Are you okay? Please pick up the phone."

No reply.

I tried calling again. Nothing.

Now, truly anxious, I messaged her once more:

"I'm sorry if I did anything wrong. Please punish me if you want to, but don't cut me off. Just give me a missed call if you're okay—even if you don't want to talk now, just let me know you're safe."

A few seconds passed. Then, a missed call.

My breath released.

Moments later, her message arrived.

"Everyone's life is messed up because of me. I'm unwanted. My own mother wishes I was dead. That bloody woman suspects me!"

Then another:

"That woman—unfortunately, my mother—screamed at me today. She thinks I spend all day chatting with boys. She doubts my character. My own

mother!"

Before I could respond, another message appeared:

"Where was she when my own relative tried to rape me? What about his character—my so-called 'Mausa'?"

I stared at the screen in disbelief. My heart ached. My fingers trembled.

I called again. She didn't answer. Instead, she messaged:

"Please... just message. I'll call later."

I typed quickly, my mind swirling:

"Babu... when did your Mausa do that? Please don't feel broken by your mother's words. I know you—your soul, your innocence. They don't understand you. They don't know the real Soumya."

She replied:

"He tried three times. Once when I was in class six, again in tenth, and the last—just seven months ago, at my youngest Mama's wedding."

"Why didn't you report him?" I asked.

"I was too young the first time—I didn't even understand what he was doing. I cried, and he left. But no one believed me. The second time, I told my mother. Instead of supporting me, she yelled at me—asked why I went near him. The third time... I slapped him. I told my youngest Mama, and he beat him up badly."

"Was he exposed? Publicly?"

"Come to Facebook," she wrote.

I logged in instantly.

She messaged:

"Who will expose him? They said it would bring shame. My Mausi's life would be ruined. That's what my mother and others said. So I was forced into silence."

I had read about such things. Reports by global agencies, studies, news articles—about how girls often aren't safe even in their own homes. But hearing it from her—my Soumya—felt like a stab in the gut. Her reality was heartbreaking.

"If he's not exposed, he'll do it again. Maybe to another girl," I replied. *"Can you give me his details?"*

"What will you do?"

"Tell me what you want me to do."

She hesitated, then wrote:

"I want him shamed among all the relatives—so he can't show his face again. But my Mausi is innocent... and his son is just two years old."

"Okay. We won't go public. But we'll collect evidence. Enough to make him afraid. So if he ever tries anything again, the fear of exposure will stop him."

She sent me his name: Navin Nanda.

"He's in my Facebook friend list," she said.

"Now, send me a smiley," I requested.

She did: ☺

"That's my Soumya," I smiled back.

"But be careful," she reminded me. *"My Mausi and the child—they're not to suffer."*

"I promise."

It was 7:17 PM. I told her I'd talk again after an hour and left the office, still burning with emotion.

On the ride home, a flood of thoughts washed over me—thoughts of how unfair this world is to girls like Soumya. From the day a girl steps into adolescence, she begins to feel unsafe. In school corridors, in public transport, on streets and in homes—everywhere, shadows follow her. She's told to adjust, to cover up, to stay quiet.

Why is it that when a girl is assaulted, she's the one asked to hide in shame?

I felt ashamed—ashamed of this world, of my own gender, of the cruelty that had wounded her so deeply.

I reached home at 8:30 PM. Picked up my usual dinner from Dalma Restaurant. After changing, I logged back into Facebook.

No calls. No messages.

I called her.

"Hello," she answered, her voice low.

"Are you okay?" I asked gently.

"Yes," she said—but it didn't sound convincing.

"I have some brain teasers for you. Super challenging ones."

She paused. *"Really? Okay, send them!"*

"Come online on Facebook."

"Alright."

I didn't have any puzzles ready, but I knew this would lift her mood. Quickly, I searched online:

"Challenging brain teasers."

Thousands popped up in an instant. I picked a few.

"First one: How can you stop a fish from smelling?"

She laughed: *"What kind of question is that?! I'm vegetarian—I don't even cook fish!"*

"So am I! But I still know the answer."

"Tell me then!"

"Cut off its nose!" ?

"Arreyyy! Hehehehehe..."

She was laughing now. And that laugh? It was all I needed to hear.

We did four more, and she nailed them all. Then she told me her WhatsApp wasn't installing on her phone. I found the right version for her Nokia model. It worked—and soon we were chatting there.

She sent me a voice note.

That voice—her voice—sweet and soft, melted all my stress.

While we were chatting, I created a fake Facebook profile: Ananya Pradhan. Used a random photo. Within minutes, I had 30 guy friends and 2 girls.

Then I found him: Navin Nanda. Same profile. Same monster. Still connected to her online.

I hit "Send Friend Request."

And I told Soumya.

CHAPTER THIRTEEN

A Message Seen, A Heart Unseen

It was 10:30 PM when I asked her gently, *"Had your dinner?"*

"No," she replied.

We agreed to take a short break and continue our conversation afterward. I finished mine within fifteen minutes, reheated leftovers I didn't really care to taste, and messaged her again on WhatsApp.

She was already online.

I waited.

My message was marked as seen—the two blue ticks, unmistakable. Still, no response. Ten minutes passed.

I typed again, something light, something just to check in.

Still nothing.

I called her.

She picked up after a few rings. Her voice was distant—composed, yet unfamiliar.

"I'm a little busy," she said. "Will talk to you later. Good night."

And the line went dead.

A short sentence. Routine, maybe. But it hit harder than a thousand silent hours.

For months, we had shared everything. Secrets. Fears. Sleepless nights. Laughter. She had become my midnight solace, the one constant presence in my uncertain days. But tonight... something had changed. WhatsApp had replaced Facebook. And I—her once dearest listener—was no longer needed.

Maybe she found someone better. Maybe he was back.

Ansh.

The name I once hoped she had erased. The one she told me had broken her, yet somehow still held the pieces.

I had no way to confirm. No right to ask. After all, we weren't in a relationship. We were "just friends." And yet, somewhere in the recess of my naïve heart, I believed we were something more. Or maybe I simply wanted us to be.

I couldn't focus. Each time I opened WhatsApp and saw her online, my heart sank a little further.

She's online. I'm online. But we're not talking.

I opened Facebook—not from my account, but from the fake profile I had created earlier: Ananya Pradhan. The digital mask I wore for a darker purpose.

It was now 11:30 PM.

Soumya was still online.

So was Navin Nanda.

A new notification blinked at the top of the page: "Friend request accepted by Navin Nanda."

Three others had accepted too. But I had eyes only for him.

My fingers hovered over the keys. I longed to tell Soumya. But what if she ignored me again?

I swallowed the ache.

Instead, Ananya sent a message:

Ananya: "Hi!!!"

He replied almost instantly.

Navin: "Hello."

Ananya: "How are you? Do we know each other?"

Navin: "I don't know. I just got a friend request from you and accepted it."

Ananya: "Oops! Must have sent it by mistake. You can unfriend me if you want."

Navin: "No...I can't."

Ananya: "Why not?"

Navin: "Who wouldn't want to be friends with a beautiful girl like you?"

Disgust swirled in my gut.

Ananya: "Thanks ☺ "

He was over twice my age—Soumya's age. Married. A father. Yet here he was, shamelessly flirting with a profile that was clearly fabricated.

Navin: "What do you do?"

Ananya: "First-year B.Tech student. You?"

Navin: "I'm working as G.M. in G.T. Infra—an infrastructure company."
His grammar bled arrogance. A infrastructure company. Right.
Ananya: "Wow! General Manager? That's impressive."
Navin: "What's your usual online time?"
Ananya: "Not fixed... but you'll usually find me here after 11 PM ☺ "
Navin: "So nice of you. I'll wait for you here at that time."
Ananya: "Sure ☺ "
Navin: "Are you in Bhubaneswar or somewhere else? My internet is slow here at Jagmohan Nagar, near ITER College Road. It's hard to chat."
Ananya: "No problem. Bye for now."
He was pathetic.

It wasn't just the flirtation. It was the intent. The entitlement. The predatory charm.

I logged out, nauseated. This was the man Soumya feared, the one who had hurt her—again and again.

I switched back to WhatsApp.

Soumya was still online.

My chest tightened.

No messages. No typing bubble. No acknowledgment.
She was just there—present, but absent. So close, yet unreachable.

My mind became a battlefield.

Brain: Stop. You're overthinking.
Heart: She's ignoring you for someone else.
Brain: You were never anything more than a friend.
Heart: But she made it feel like more.
Brain: She never promised anything.
Heart: Then why did she make me feel special?

For once, the brain won.

I decided I would pull away. Not out of ego, but for self-preservation. It would be painful, but it was necessary.

I turned off my laptop. Got into bed at **2:47 AM.**

I tried to sleep.

But her memories clung to me—her voice, her smile, her pain. The tsunami of emotions refused to quieten.

On impulse, I opened WhatsApp again.

Her status read: "Last seen at 3:14 AM."

Just five minutes ago.

For reasons I couldn't explain, that calmed me.

And eventually, I drifted off.

61

CHAPTER FOURTEEN

Mornings Without Her

Morning came heavy. Not with work, not with noise—but with silence. The kind that throbbed just behind the ears when you're waiting for a message that won't come.

I checked my phone. Nothing.
WhatsApp last seen: 8:34 AM.

I had expected a call from her. Just a little "good morning," or even a missed call. But the screen stayed still. Cold. She had been online, and yet...

I broke my own rule.

I called her.

Busy.

I forced myself to smile. Typed "Good Morning" and walked out, heading to the office like I wasn't falling apart inside. My body was at work, but my mind... it was stuck on a 5.5-inch screen, waiting for a message that wouldn't beep.

She hadn't even replied to that—not the night before, not this morning. And we were friends? Were we?

No. I was a fool. Expecting warmth from a heart that had clearly gone cold.

At 4:00 PM, she called.

I let it ring.

Strange how someone you crave talking to suddenly feels unworthy of your voice—not out of ego, but to give them a taste of what they gave you: absence.

She called again.

This time, I couldn't resist.

"Good morning," she chirped, almost too happy.

But her voice—something was missing. The warmth. The spark. The sweetness I used to recognize even in her yawns. I replied flatly.

"Hello."

She paused.

"When you don't want to talk, then fine. Bye."

The line cut. Abrupt. Like my feelings didn't matter. Like the pain she caused was invisible to her.

I said *"bye"*—and regretted it immediately.

Every time my phone buzzed, I hoped it was her. But nothing came. No message. No missed call. Just the hollow ring of silence.

And again, the battle began.

Brain: She ignored you. She should say sorry.

Heart: She's younger. Show some maturity.

Brain: She lied to you. Over and over.

Heart: She's in love. And everything is fair in love and war.

This time, the heart won.

I picked up my phone and messaged her on Facebook:

"I miss you."

Then I logged out.

Thirty minutes later, the phone rang.

Her name flashed across the screen.

"Hello."

"Hello. I'm sorry," I whispered before I could overthink it.

"You're pagal... forget that! Tell me—what's up?" she beamed.

I melted. As if her voice could patch all broken things.

"Nothing special... I was missing you."

"Awww, sachi? I've been dying to tell you so many things. I wanted to talk, but you were naraz!"

("Aww, really? There's so much I've been wanting to tell you. I missed talking to you... but you were angry with me.")

"I'm in office. I'll call you once I'm home."

"Ok bbye!"

"Bye."

And just like that, the world felt balanced again.

CHAPTER FIFTEEN

PLANS, PREGNANCIES, AND PROMISES

At home, I called her.

"Hello."

"Hi."

"What's up?"

"Nothing. Just music."

Then she dropped a bomb.

"Guess what? Anisha's pregnant."

I blinked. *"Who's Anisha?"*

"My +2 friend. Her boyfriend's doing a job. He's 8 years older than her!"

Irresponsible fools, I thought.

"Her parents took her to some remote place. Probably for an abortion."

"Right decision," I said bluntly, not wanting to linger on the topic.

"But what about the child? What was his fault?"

None.

But this wasn't about the child. This was about life choices, consequences, maturity.

We drifted away from the topic. Tried to scrape up more conversation.

"I forgot to tell you... your mausa ji—he's been messaging Ananya a lot lately."

She laughed.

"Really? He'll start flirting again. Dirty talks incoming, I bet!"

"He's already started. I'll trap him. You'll see."

"Can I see the chats? Give me the ID and password?"

"Not yet. I'll give it to you later."

"Okay."

Then her voice changed—bubbly, mischievous.

"Only five days to my result, na?"

"Even I'm counting the days."

"There's a surprise for you."

"Tell me!"

"Tomorrow."

"At least a hint?"

"Nope."

And with that, she told me to log into Facebook. She missed watching mausa ji squirm.

On Facebook, she greeted me with a long:

"Hiiiiiiiiiiiiiiii"

Then, casually:

"We're going to Bangalore in June!"

Why?

"Family trip. Then Kerala. Every year we go."

"Oh..."

"Papa and Mummy are doing the Art of Living course for five days. They'll be in full silence—no phones, no communication. I'll be totally free."

I raised an eyebrow at the screen.

"So?"

"So... I had a plan. If you could come to Bangalore..."

Did she mean... just us?

"WHAT? Masti?"

"Exactly."

I laughed. "Your parents will kill me!"

"Pagalu ho! They'll be in different rooms, meditating for five days. I'll be free like a bird. Just you and me—in a new city!"

She painted a picture of freedom, laughter, food, movies... full-on masti.

I wanted it. More than I could admit. Even though I knew her heart wasn't mine. Even though Dubai awaited me in May for business.

Still—I wanted to be with her. To escape everything else.

"Are you sure there won't be problems?"

"Nothing will happen. I guarantee it. Pakka."

She was excited. When she was excited, her Hindi poured out like a child's storybook.

"Reservation done?"

"Yes. Rajdhani, 10th May."

"Okay. I'll book in another train for the same date."

"Book today! Or no ticket."

"Tomorrow, pakka."

She giggled. "Now check what mausa ji is doing!"

I switched to Ananya Pradhan.

Navin:

"Hai sweety. U again online at 1.09AM wow.

I might got that power to be online at 2.00 PM, but after office I become sleepy...

I am usually online at 11.00AM to 5.00PM.

*Off: 9861***991."*

I shook my head.

His English was a crime.

His intentions? Even worse.

And yet... this is what Soumya had been protecting me from. And herself.

Ananya:

"Thank u. I'm still studying... so I don't want any job right now. After my B.Tech, I'm planning for MBA."

Navin:

"So nice of u, sweety. Good planning... Are you staying in a hostel or your house? In which area?

You know... without seeing any chat message, I feel a little worried. But when I see something... it makes me smile. Like your photo—you're smiling in that."

Ananya:

"I'm staying in a hostel. In Patia."

Navin:

"So nice... I've also done my MBA in Finance from Berhampur University. Your decision is good."

Ananya:

"Thank you, sir. Bye. Feeling sleepy."

Navin:

"Bye... it was nice chatting with you."

I couldn't help it. I had to share it with Soumya.

Me: "Your mausaji is going mad for me. He calls me sweety ?. Such a romantic person... you know? And for such a nice man, you think so badly? ?"

Soumya: "Shut up..."

Me: "No, I'm serious. He's showing real interest in me. Such a bastard—his wife must be sleeping next to him, and here he is, flirting with someone who's less than half his age!"

Soumya: "This is nothing! Just start talking about the stuff every guy dreams of hearing from a girl. Then watch his actions and reactions."

Me: "I won't talk rubbish. He'll initiate all that on his own—I'm pretty sure."

Soumya: "Yes, I know. Acha suno(listen)... It's 2:00 AM. I need to get up early tomorrow."

Me: "Why?"

Soumya: "I'll tell you later. It's part of the surprise!"

Me: "Okay then. Sleep well. Bye. Good night."

Soumya: "Bye. Good night. Take care."

I logged out of Facebook, but not from her thoughts.

Everything was okay.

Still, a strange uneasiness began to spread through me—like a silent tide pulling me into unknown depths. I couldn't name it fully then, but I knew it had something to do with the fear of losing her.

We talked so much. Shared so many things. Teased. Cared. But still... she wasn't mine.

She had Ansh.

And I—I was falling, helplessly.

Despite knowing her heart belonged elsewhere, I couldn't stop feeling the way I did. That night, I told myself once this mausa ji issue was dealt with, **I'd pull back. Keep some emotional distance. Stay sane.**

But another voice inside me whispered something else.

If she truly loves Ansh... then why did she invite me to Bangalore?

Why plan days alone together?

Why want me to be the one to share her freedom?

Was she confused? Torn between the emotional stability I gave and the romantic chaos Ansh brought? Or was I just reading too much into the crumbs she dropped?

I didn't know.

But what I did know—what scared me the most—was that I couldn't imagine a Bangalore without her. **Or a life where she was just another friend.**

And that meant I was already too far in.

PUPPETS AND PUPPETEERS

Saturday. 9:25 AM.

No office today. No meetings. No distractions. Just one desire burning in my chest like a morning sun—I wanted to talk to her.

I wanted to hear her voice—the soft musical tone that stayed with me long after our conversations ended. But sometimes, it's not just about hearing them. It's about them wanting to hear you too. You crave to be missed. Not because of ego, but because of something gentler... something called self-worth.

10:00 AM. Still no call. No message. Nothing.

I finally gave in.

Hi, I messaged her on WhatsApp.

One tick.

No second tick.

No delivery.

Her internet must be off. Or her phone. I tried again—an SMS this time. "Good Morning!"

Delivered.

And yet... 30 minutes passed. Still nothing.

My mind spun its worst theories. Was she on call with Ansh?

And with that, the old battle between my heart and brain flared up again:

Brain: She must be talking with Ansh.

Heart: No. Maybe she's studying.

Brain: Then why hasn't she replied to your SMS?

Heart: Maybe she's out of balance. Or asleep. Or... anything but Ansh.

Eventually, both sides—heart and brain—agreed on one thing:
Call her.

I pressed her name. Let it ring. 10... 12 times. No answer.

I sighed.

Maybe her parents were around.

Beep."Do not call. Papa is here. I will call you later."

Relief. Warm and rushing. I sat back, guilt washing away.

Meanwhile, I had another mission.

I logged into Ananya Pradhan's account.

Navin was online.

Navin: Hi Sweety ..How R U ?

Perfect timing.

This wasn't just casual chat anymore. I wanted to test him. Corner him. Break his illusion of decency.

Ananya: Hi... I'm great!! Thanks for asking. I need an urgent help from you...

Hook.

He bit.

And the rest unraveled like a sick, predictable script—Navin exposing the depths of his depravity with every reply.

I watched him cross line after line with disturbing comfort. A 39-year-old married man—begging for pictures, talking of kisses, hugs, private parks, and "puppies."

And here I was, using words I had learned from Soumya—her teenage slang, her girlish emojis, her sweetly dangerous tone—to pull out the truth from a man pretending to be mature, respectable, and married.

"Tum mujhe bahut pasand ho..." ("I really like you...")

"Main tumhe baahon mein bhar leta..." ("I would hold you in my arms...")

"Tumhari photo us profile me, kisi ko bhi ghayal kar sakti hai..." ("Your photo in that profile could wound anyone's heart...")

Sickening.

He was ready to ruin a life over a few sweet words and a fake photo.

And if I wasn't pretending—if I were a real girl named Ananya—then this man could have destroyed me.

I logged out.

Disgusted.

And yet, a colder silence was waiting for me on the other side.

Still no word from Soumya.

Not a call. Not a message. Not even a "Hi."

The only message she had sent me all day was that one, earlier in the morning.

And now?

4:00 PM.

I hadn't eaten. Hadn't moved much.

My stomach growled. My mind fogged.

And my heart... it ached—not for Ananya, not for the mission, not even for justice.

But for Soumya.

All I wanted was to talk to her.

Tell her everything.

About Navin.

About what I'd done.

About how badly I missed her.

But she was silent.

And silence was louder than anything Navin could have ever typed.

CHAPTER SEVENTEEN

THE SURPRISE

It was 7:00 PM.

Hitesh messaged me, asking if I'd join him and Dhiraj for dinner.

It was Saturday — our regular dinner night.

That evening, we had plans to dine at a well-known restaurant in I.D. Market, Nayapalli. Hitesh asked me to be there by 9:00 PM — two hours from now.

But I was deeply missing her.

I was craving the sound of her voice — that musical tone that made everything feel alright. I wanted to have a silly conversation, just to feel close to her. Beyond all that, I needed to talk to her about the latest updates in Mausaji's case. But there had been no message from her. Every time my phone beeped, I hoped it was her. Each time it rang, I prayed it was her call. I must have checked my phone a hundred times, just to see her online status on WhatsApp or Facebook. But her last seen was still 16 hours ago.

I couldn't take it anymore. I picked up my phone, opened the message box, and typed:

"I miss you so badly, babu... please give me a missed call if you're okay but unable to talk."

Moments after the message was delivered, I got a missed call from her. A wave of relief washed over me. She was okay — probably just with her parents and unable to call. I had to get ready for dinner now. I quickly showered, then hopped on my bike toward Hitesh's place. Dhiraj was already there. As usual, the three of us squeezed onto a single bike and headed to Rainbow Restaurant. On the way, Hitesh and Dhiraj grabbed cigarettes from a roadside shop. We reached the restaurant by 8:30 PM.

We ordered butter naan, Kadhai Paneer, fried rice, and Chicken 65. Dhiraj, the only non-vegetarian among us, ordered the chicken. The food took about 30 minutes, so we spent the time chatting.

Hitesh brought up the **U.A.E.** visa. He suggested that he and I should go to **Dubai** while Dhiraj managed the office here. But I knew Dhiraj secretly wanted to go too. Though he didn't openly object, his body language said enough. And while I had every reason to be in **Dubai** — being the one who usually made all key decisions — my heart was still in Bangalore... with Soumya. It was one of those moments when leadership means stepping back, not forward.

So I said, "Hitesh, I think you and Dhiraj should go. Dhiraj's a great designer. Seeing the site firsthand will give him a better understanding of the theme. He needs this exposure. I can manage the office here."

Hitesh was quiet, but Dhiraj looked genuinely happy. A few minutes later, Hitesh said, "It's fine if Dhiraj goes... but if you came too, that would be even better."

Hitesh wasn't giving up easily. But this time, Dhiraj stepped in and supported me, repeating my reasoning. Finally, Hitesh agreed to go with Dhiraj.

By 9:40 PM, our food was served, and conversation gave way to silence as we focused on the delicious meal. Sometimes, good food can ease even the heaviest of hearts — and for a little while, I forgot how much I missed Soumya. I took it as a small personal victory.

It was 10:15 PM when we finished. Hitesh and Dhiraj lit their Gold Flake Lights before we all rode back. I dropped them off and reached my place around 11:00 PM.

Fifteen minutes later, I got a message from Soumya:

"Open the door, quick!!"

I immediately called her.

"Which door? Where are you?"

"Pehle apna door to kholo, pagal!" she giggled. ("Open your door first, you crazy!" she giggled.)

I opened the door — and there she was. In a pink T-shirt, smiling mischievously.

"SURRRRRRRRRRPRIZZZZZZZZZZZE!!"

She had that special way of saying "Surprise" that made me feel like the most important person in the world.

"When did you arrive?" I asked.

"Just now. And I came straight to see you," she said sweetly.

"What about your parents? Won't they wonder why you're out so late?"

"I told them I had to call a friend to ask about result dates. They must think I'm still on the phone." She giggled again.

"Wow... you came just to see me, na?"

"Noooo... ummm... Yes."

"Pagal! Now go home, get fresh, and come online, okay?"

"Five minutes, please... let me talk to you." she pleaded.

"I'll talk the whole night if you ask... but it's risky here. Let's talk at the window, okay?"

"Okay... see you in 30 minutes at my window." She smiled mischievously.

After a long wait of 35 minutes , she finally messaged me:

"Come to the window, quickly!"

I was already there. Without delay, I slid open the glass pane. What I saw deserves a little description.

There she was—phone in hand, typing something. She wore a long, sleeveless red ganji that barely reached her thighs. Her hair was falling onto her face, swayed by the fan blowing at full speed. And in that moment, she looked like the most beautiful girl in the world. I was completely lost in her charm, mesmerized by the way she looked while just existing. She looked breathtaking.

Suddenly, my phone vibrated. It was her, calling.

"Hello?" I answered.

"Where are you?" she asked.

"Right opposite your window, watching you for the last five minutes," I chuckled.

"Liar! You can't see me—I'm sitting at the corner," she protested.

"I still can. Look at my window—you'll see my phone's light."

I waved my hand and showed her my phone's light.

"Turn your light on—I want to see you!" she said.

I switched on the room light. She spotted me and waved, saying "Hi" with the cutest smile. We were still on the phone, even while seeing each other.

I suggested we talk directly, but she refused—her mother was asleep in the next room.

We decided to continue over the phone, seeing each other through the windows.

"It's been so long since we saw each other, hasn't it?" she said.
"Yes... and tonight is the happiest night of my life," I replied.
"Night, not day," she corrected.
"Okay, okay... happy now?" I teased.

Then, she said it—so innocently and unknowingly seductive:
"It feels like our first wedding night..."
I laughed.
*"Really? We're ten feet apart—how could we possibly do *those* things?"*

"Shut up! I didn't mean it like that!" she said, flustered.

I couldn't resist teasing her.
She blushed, and her cheeks turned red.

Then she said,
"Wait... I want to send you something. Come to WhatsApp."

I ended the call and opened WhatsApp immediately.

She sent a few pictures—gorgeous ones from her mama's place. In one, she was wearing a wedding dress, adorned in jewelry. She looked divine. Not just beautiful—goddess-like. So pure, I felt like even touching her would ruin her perfection. I was completely captivated. And for a moment... I felt jealous of Ansh.

My feelings were growing stronger—an undeniable desire to love her... to be hers.

"How are the pictures?" she asked.

I had no words.

"You're beautiful," I typed.

*"And you're pagalu—*my* pagalu,"* she replied, sweet as ever.

That word—"my"—struck deep. She *claimed* me, even in a small way. I felt something shift inside me.

I wrote:
"Babu, I missed you so much."
"Aww, really?"
"Yes, a lot."
"Babu missed her pagalu soooo much too!"

I couldn't hold back anymore:
"You're my Babu... my Soumya. I won't let you go again."

"When did you fall so in love with me?" she teased.
"Since many lifetimes ago," I replied.
"Hehehe... Pagalu," she giggled.
"I'm serious," I messaged.

She paused.
"I want to confess something," she said.

"Okay... go ahead."
"I wanted to hug you that day... but you told me to leave because it was too risky even to talk."

Her words stunned me. She felt the same.

"Babu, I'm sorry. It was really risky that day," I admitted.
"But I want to confess something too—only if you promise not to mind."
"Pagal... I'll never mind. Just say it."
"Umm... leave it."
"No drama. Say it."
"I... I also wanted to hug you"

"Awww! Then why didn't you, stupid!?"

"I don't know... but now, I want to."

She looked at me from her window, and our eyes met—just for a second. But it said everything. There was desire in her eyes... the same that was raging in my heart.

She messaged:

"I want it too. Can you hug me now?"

"How? You're ten feet away and two concrete walls in between."

"Then break those walls," she replied mischievously.

"Pagal... we'll hug tomorrow."

"No—now. I have a risky idea," she said.

She explained her plan—how her parents were too tired to wake up, and how she'd lock them in from outside.
She was serious.

"Babu... it's too risky."

"No risk, no fun. And I like a little madness," she insisted.

"Are you really coming?"

"Wait. Let me check if the coast is clear."

I was scared. Scared something would go wrong. Scared Dr. Patra might find out. Scared of hurting her trust—or mine.

Then she called me.

"Keep the door open. Soumya is coming!"

"You're welcome,"I replied and opened the door.

Within five minutes, she arrived—wrapped in a bedsheet, smiling.

"WHHHHOOOOAAA!" she giggled.

"Aren't you scared?" I asked.
"I was. Not anymore."

"And this bedsheet?" I laughed.

"I didn't feel like changing at this hour!" she said sweetly.

She wanted to see my room—the one opposite hers. She climbed the stairs. I followed.

"What's the mission now?" I joked.

"You're too eager to hug me... shameless!" she laughed.

"Pagal, I just want you to leave safely—it's risky."

"You think too much. I love that about you,"she smiled.

"Let's hug," I said, sincerely.

"Finally! That's what I wanted to hear, stupid."

She unwrapped the bedsheet—and suddenly, I was weak. She looked so sensual, so tempting, it was hard to keep control. I avoided her gaze.

"I don't know how to hug a girl," I confessed. "You start."

"You're my pagalu... totally mad."

She stepped closer, took my hands, placed them on her waist, and hugged me. My arms moved from her waist to her back, and I pulled her close. Our hearts were racing—together.

No fear. Just warmth.

She laid her head on my chest. We stayed like that, silent but alive.

And then... I saw her lips—pink, perfect, like rose petals.

I don't know who moved first, but her lips touched mine. Sweet. Warm. Real.

We kissed.

At first, 20 seconds.

Then we laughed.

Then, again.

This time, longer—passionate, deep. We kissed for 15 minutes, though it felt like hours.

And then I whispered in her ear:

"Soumya, I need to confess something... I've loved you since I first saw you. I love you for who you are. I'll keep loving you for who you'll become. My love will grow with every second. I breathe for you."
She said nothing. Just slowly wrapped herself in the bedsheet again and left.

It was 2:20 AM.

I called. No answer.

I messaged. No reply.

I kept trying. Still nothing.

Then came a message:

"I want to confess something.
I know you might be angry, but I have to be honest.
I lied—I haven't broken up with Ansh.
I'm still with him. I still love him more than anything.
He's busy with exams—that's why we talk less.

But... I like you. I trust you. When I'm in trouble, you're the first name that comes to mind. I call you without thinking.

Thank you for always being there.
I don't know what compelled me to hug you today. I should've stopped myself.

And even more... we kissed.
It was the most beautiful moment of my life.
Yes, it was cheating on Ansh.
But I don't regret it.

You're the most wonderful person I've known. But I can't betray him.

Please understand.
Please forgive me.
Please forget everything that happened today.
And please... be my friend forever.

Bye. Good night."

I was shattered.

Just like that, she dismissed it all as an "accident".

How could she?

Why didn't she ever hint that I was just a backup?

How can someone be this cruel?

I didn't know what to reply. I just wrote:
"Bye."

It was 3:30 AM.

But sleep wouldn't come. My brain had shut down. I tried not to think about her.
But how do you stop thinking about someone who's become a habit?
How do you unlove someone who once made you feel like the most special soul alive?

CHAPTER EIGHTEEN

Sweety, I'll Ruin You

23 April 2014 – Morning, 9:17 AM

My phone beeped—a good morning text from her. But no call. That was unusual. Her voice had become part of my morning ritual. I replied simply, **"Good Morning."** Part of me was relieved she had messaged. But I missed her voice.

I brushed with one hand and scrolled my phone with the other, hoping she'd call.

To distract myself, I logged into the Ananya Pradhan Facebook account. Seventeen new messages. Seven from her mausaji, Navin. The rest were from random boys.

Navin's messages:

"You didn't reply, sweety."
"Send me your latest pic in jeans."
"I can't sleep thinking about you."

A surge of anger and disgust rushed through me. I immediately tried to call her.

"The number you are trying to call is currently busy."

I waited, then tried again after thirty minutes—still busy.

It's one of the worst feelings—when the person you're dying to talk to is busy talking to someone else.

At work, I couldn't focus. I wasn't the same anymore. I was addicted to her voice, her presence—her.

By 8:00 PM, my phone rang. It was her. I let it ring. Once. Twice. On the second try, I picked up.

Me: "So, what's up?"
Soumya: "Nothing much, just listening to music."
Me: "I wanted to talk about your mausaji. We need to expose him."

Soumya: "Send me the ID and password. I'll handle it."

She reminded me her Class 12 board results and NISER entrance exam were tomorrow. Before I could respond, the call dropped. I called her back. Still busy.

Frustrated, I deleted her number from my contacts, cleared the messages and call logs. I told myself I was done.

But within the hour, I missed her again.

I logged into Facebook and messaged her there, sending the Ananya credentials. Then I began scrolling through our old chats. One from 10 Feb 2014, when she had messaged me from her mom's account, made me smile:

"Kal course mein aajana chupchaap, nahi to gunde bhej dungi ?!!"

("Come to the course quietly tomorrow... or I'll send goons after you!! ?")

But the smile didn't last. Navin was online again.

From Ananya's profile, I sent:

Ananya: "Hi."

Navin: "Sweety! I missed you. Can't wait till Sunday."

Ananya: "Even I'm counting the days."

Navin: "I want to kiss you... your lips."

Ananya: "Send me your nude pic first."

Navin: "You first."

Ananya: "I don't have a phone. You go first."

After some hesitation, he sent it. Disgusting. But now we had what we needed.

I texted her on Facebook:

"Call me ASAP. Urgent."

Back on chat:

Ananya: "Your wife would know better."

Navin: "She's all loose now. I want a bubbly girl like you..."

Ananya: "You have two options—confess, or I'll ruin you."

Navin: "Who are you??"

Ananya: "The one you tried to exploit. Your game's over."

He vanished. Within minutes, his profile was wiped clean. Coward.

She called—thrilled, relieved, grateful. She thanked me again and again. Said she would show the screenshots to her family.

For the first time in days, we talked the way we used to. For a while, it felt like us again.

Around 2:00 AM, she whispered that she needed to sleep.

That night, I wrote in my diary:

"Kab kaha ki tu mujhse muhabbat kar le,
Gair na ban tu... bas itni si khwahish to hai..."
(I never asked you to love me.
Just not to become a stranger—that's all I ever wished.)

CHAPTER NINETEEN

FALLING APART, HOLDING ON

24 April 2014 – A Day That Felt Different

Today felt different—for two reasons. First, because her board exam results were being announced. And second, because after what felt like ages, I was genuinely happy. There was something in the air—perhaps hope, perhaps a sense of purpose. Also, Hitesh and Dhiraj were expected to receive their work visas for Dubai today, making it a big day for them too.

The first thing I did after waking up was power on my laptop.

It was only 8:00 AM, but I couldn't wait to check her results. I sent her a message:

"All the best for today's exam."

I opened the Odisha board website and saw a notice:

"Results to be published at 10:00 AM."

I called Hitesh. He asked if I could come along to collect their visas and also wanted me to help prepare the presentation for our Dubai client. Honestly, I hadn't done any of it yet. But I told him it was ready—I just needed to review it before sending. I also excused myself from going with him, pretending I had some urgent personal work.

After a quick bath and breakfast, I kept the laptop open, checking the time again and again. At 9:30 AM, I felt the same nervous energy as if I were awaiting my own board exam results—curious, anxious, hopeful. I wished she were with me to check her result together, but I knew she was appearing for her NISER exam today.

At exactly 10:00 AM, I entered her roll number and date of birth.

69.67%

Not even 70.

I wasn't exactly shocked, but I hadn't expected it to be that low either. Just a year ago, she had scored 95.5%! I couldn't help but think of **Ansh**—how her focus had shifted since he entered her life. *Love is meant to uplift, not derail. A true partner supports growth, not distraction. He was already studying in a top engineering college. He knew how important this exam was for her. Why didn't he guide her? Why didn't he insist she study instead of being constantly online with him? I was furious—but I had no right to say anything.*

Outside, I was calm. Inside, a storm raged.

I cancelled my plan to go to the office. I knew she would need someone, and I wanted to be there for her.

At 2:20 PM, she called.

Soumya: "Where are you?"

Me: "I'm in my room today."

She hung up.

Five minutes later, she came to see me. Her face said everything. She looked devastated. And strangely, I felt as though I had received those marks.

Soumya: "Papa's not answering my call. He's disappointed."

Her voice trembled. That pain—it tore through me. She hadn't even shed a tear, but I could feel how broken she was inside.

Me: "Hey, your result isn't bad at all. The entire board's performance dropped this year. I read about it in the papers. Your papa must be busy, that's all. Don't worry—everything's going to be fine. Trust me, okay?"

My attempt to console her broke her composure. Tears welled in her eyes. She didn't say anything. I stood up and gently pulled her into a hug. She buried her face into my shoulder, sobbing.

Soumya: "I've ruined my future... and my parents' trust."

I held her tighter and whispered:

"Soumya, this is just a result. And it's not even bad. Your JEE and NISER results are still pending. No single exam decides your future. Dhirubhai Ambani wasn't from IIT, and he didn't top in school either. There are countless examples like that. Main hoon na... sab theek ho jaayega.(*"I'm here for you... it'll all be fine."*)"

I felt the shift—she was no longer crying.

Soumya: "Pakka sab theek ho jaayega na?" (*"Everything will be fine for sure, right?"*)

Me: "Yes, pakka." (*"Yes, for sure."*)

I asked her to have lunch, but she said she wanted one more hug. I felt like the luckiest man alive. We stood there for five minutes in silence, holding each other. Then we heard footsteps. Someone was coming. We quickly pulled away, just as her mother entered.

She asked her to come for lunch. I tried to cover up the situation and said to her mom:

"Aunty, please don't worry about the marks. This year's board results were generally poor. Even the topper scored just 85.7%. And trust me—Soumya is still one of the brightest students I know."

Her mother didn't say much but left with Soumya.

A couple of minutes later, my phone buzzed with a message from her:

Soumya:

"Thank you... for changing my mood and for the hug. Thank you for being there when I needed you the most. Sorry too—I know my result hurt you as well."

Me:

"Pagal, have your lunch and get some rest. You must be tired."

Soumya:

"hmmm...ok"

[Then another message]

"Thank you for everything."

Me:

"Now this one for what?"

Soumya:

"For my result. No one cared whether I was happy or upset. But you... you were always there. You encouraged me to study when I had no motivation. This result—whatever it is—is only because of you. Thank you again."

Me:

"Pagal... jyada dialogues mat maaro. And go eat your lunch now. Bye."

("Stop being dramatic, you crazy. Go have your lunch now. Bye.")

CHAPTER TWENTY

DEALS AND DAMAGES

A Turning Point – Personally and Professionally

It was a good day. Hitesh and Dhiraj had received their flight tickets to Dubai from our client. They were set to leave in five days. Though a bit nervous, they were equally excited. This trip was more than just business—it was a major opportunity. A big assignment awaited us in Dubai, one that could completely transform the future of our company. This was the kind of project that could open doors we hadn't even imagined yet.

We were deep in discussion, going over the trip details and the strategic plan when my phone buzzed. It was a message from her:

Soumya:

"If you're free, please come on Facebook."

I wasn't free, but it didn't matter. No matter how busy I was, I could never miss a chance to talk to her. I made up an excuse and postponed the meeting to the evening.

Once they left, I logged into Facebook. She was already online.

My inbox was full of messages from her—along with several screenshots. She had sent me parts of a conversation between Ansh and some girl. It was disturbing.

Soumya:

"What is all this? I loved him truly, and this is what he does... that haramkhor(scoundrel)!"

I looked at the screenshots. They were indeed shocking. Ansh had been having extremely inappropriate conversations with another girl. They were even sharing semi-nude photos. There were dozens of these screenshots—there was no room for doubt.

Soumya:

"When he wanted to talk dirty, I always refused... Is this my punishment? Am I so stupid to have trusted him?"

Me:

"Soumya, please listen... I'm calling you."

Soumya:

"No, not now. Call me later."

Me:

"Soumya, I know how these college guys are. Most of them get into relationships just to pass time during their engineering years. You may have loved him sincerely—but he never intended to take it seriously."

Soumya:

"But why me?"

Me:

"Because you were too innocent, and that made you an easy target. That's all."

Soumya:

"I always stood by him. Even during my exams, when he was stressed, I gave him all my time. Is this the reward for being loyal?"

Me:

"Please try to stay calm... there could still be a misunderstanding. Did you try talking to him?"

Soumya:

"I sent him all the screenshots. He saw them—and ignored me. Didn't even reply. I guess I'm no longer of any use to him."

Me:

"Soumya, don't overthink. Just breathe. Some people simply don't understand the value of trust. Maybe he's one of them."

I could feel her pain. Her trust was shattered. Her voice might have been silent behind the screen, but I knew she was crying. Strangely, amid all this, a part of me felt a sense of relief. I don't know why—maybe because the truth had finally come out. Maybe because she now saw what I had always feared.

I tried calling her to comfort her, but she didn't answer. She logged off from Facebook.

An hour later, I tried again. Still no response. I began to worry.

That evening, I had to sit with Hitesh and Dhiraj to go over the Dubai business plan. But I knew I couldn't focus unless I was sure Soumya was okay.

I tried once more—and this time, she picked up.

She told me she had tried calling Ansh, but he didn't answer. Instead, one of his friends picked up. The audacity of it—his friend casually told her not to worry and even said that he was there for her if Ansh cheated. What an opportunist!

Me:

"Give me his number. I'll talk to him."

Soumya:

"No, there's no need. I'll only talk to Ansh if he calls and shows genuine regret. Only then I'll consider whether this relationship is worth continuing."

There was a new tone in her voice—firmness. She wasn't smiling, but at least she wasn't breaking down anymore. That gave me peace.

I told her about my upcoming meeting and that it might take an hour or two. She assured me that she would be okay.

For the first time in a long while, I saw a glimpse of strength in her eyes—and that was enough for me to get through the rest of the evening.

CHAPTER TWENTY-ONE

THE MOST IMPORTANT SUNDAY

5:30 PM, UniSys Solutions, Bhubaneswar Office

Hitesh:

"Did you read the client's email?"

Me:

"Yes, he wants a full roadmap for renovating their existing system."

Hitesh:

"And you're not coming with us to Dubai? What's so urgent in Bangalore that you're skipping your dream trip?"

Me:

"I'm sorry, Hitesh. I'll explain everything soon. But trust me, this Bangalore trip is crucial—maybe the most important one in my life. Please understand."

Hitesh:

"I get it. But what do I tell the client? Any excuse can hurt our reputation, and you know that."

Me:

"I'll be constantly available. And if something urgent arises, I'll join you in Dubai. I only need five days in Bangalore."

Hitesh:

"Alright. That sounds fair."

We moved on to planning our client proposal—brainstorming, strategizing, and documenting a compelling pitch. Around 8:30 PM, we packed up dinner from a nearby place and called it a day.

As I got home, I noticed three missed calls and a message from Soumya:

Soumya:

"Where are you??"

I texted back:
"Reaching there in 30 minutes."
  9:30 PM, My Room
  Soumya:
"I'm scared... strange feeling."
  Me:
"Scared of what?"
  Soumya:
"I don't know. It happens sometimes... even back in the hostel."
  Me:
"Babu, you don't need to be scared. I'm with you. Always."
  Soumya:
"Thank you for always supporting me."
  Me:
"Can we continue chatting after dinner?"
  Soumya:
"Please don't go anywhere right now. I'm really scared."
  Me:
"Can I call you?"
  Soumya:
"Okay."

To distract her from that anxious feeling, I shared jokes and fun quiz questions. She answered all of them brilliantly—her laughter slowly replacing her fear. When I asked if she had dinner, she said she didn't feel like eating. I insisted, and finally she agreed—but only on the condition that I stay available after dinner. That made me feel strangely lucky.

11:05 PM – She Called Again

She began by asking if I was free, knowing I usually worked late. But what she didn't know was that if she wanted to talk, I'd always be free.

She spoke about Ansh again. About how he'd hurt her, how he'd also once made her feel special—singing songs, playing the guitar. Her voice—so raw, so real—felt like music to my ears. I quietly recorded it... it felt like preserving a piece of a dream.

She trusted me enough to open up without filters. I listened as if every word was a song I never wanted to forget. I shared some funny stories from my own life, which made her laugh. That laughter—I'd do anything to keep hearing it.

She mentioned her JEE result was due the next day and she was nervous about it. We ended up talking the entire night—until 5:15 AM.

A New Morning

You can't imagine how it feels to wake up to someone's "Good Morning" before your eyes are even open. To know someone waited for you to wake up—just to talk.

After 30 days, I woke up to a call from Soumya. She was still in bed, teasing me:

Soumya:

"Kumbhakaran!"

I laughed and told her to get fresh, have breakfast, and come over. It was Sunday—no office. And I had planned this Sunday just for her.

Late Morning – At My Place

She arrived, holding a badminton racket.

Me:

"Why the racket?"

Soumya:

"We're going to play badminton!"

Me:

"Where? In the gallery? You know boys live in the opposite building. I don't want them staring at you."

Soumya:

"Aww... jealous, are we? =D"

Me:

"Maybe. But I won't play... and I won't let you play with anyone else either."

Soumya:

"Fine! Then no studying today. Let's watch a movie on your laptop."

Me:

"Good idea. But what will you tell your mom?"

Soumya:

"Ohh, your Sasumaa(mother-in-law)! You're so scared of her!"

Why does she say "Sasumaa" so casually? Doesn't she realize the storm it stirs in my heart?

Before I could reply, she tied her hair into a bun and said:

Soumya:

"Mumma and Papa have gone shopping for our trip. Don't worry."

She entered my room like she owned the space. Sat on my chair. Switched on my laptop.

Soumya:

"Password?"

No one had ever dared to ask me for that. But to her, it was her right. I gave it without a second thought.

She browsed through my folders, mischievously claiming she'd expose my 'truth.' She wasn't even letting me touch the laptop now. I just watched, amused.

Soumya:

"What kind of boy are you? Nothing interesting in here. Trash this laptop!"

I burst out laughing.

Soumya:

"Stop grinning. Where are the movies, Mr. Saint?"

I handed her my external hard drive.

Soumya:

"Ah! Hiding the good stuff, huh?"

She plugged it in and exclaimed:

Soumya:

"You have The Blue Lagoon! I've been looking for this for years!"

Me:

"Please don't watch that..."

Soumya:

"Now I have to watch it. Sit down and shut up."

She ordered. I obeyed.

We laughed through the movie—especially during the awkward scenes—throwing silly jokes and giggling like kids. It wasn't the movie; it was us. I felt like the happiest person alive. All because of her—Soumya.

Afternoon

After the movie, she said she should leave—her parents could return any minute. Just as we reached the gate, she noticed my bike.

Soumya:

"Will you teach me how to ride?"

Me:

"Of course! Let's start now."

Soumya:

"Now??"

Me:

"Yes. You already ride a scooty. You'll get it quickly."

I explained the clutch, gears, brakes. She was nervous—manual bikes were new to her. But she got it. She moved a few meters in first gear. Her eyes lit up like a child's.

Me:

"Ask your mumma if she'll allow it. We'll go somewhere open to practice."

She agreed happily.

Just then, her parents pulled up in their Swift Dzire. She left the bike and ran toward them, waving. I watched from the gate, smiling, then walked back inside.

CHAPTER TWENTY-TWO

A RIDE TO REMEMBER

It was 5:30 PM. Hitesh and Dhiraj were both in my room, and the atmosphere was light, filled with laughter and plans. Before their much-awaited trip to Dubai, Hitesh wanted to buy a new phone. I casually suggested an Indian brand—Micromax.

"Micromax? Seriously? Poor quality," Hitesh dismissed immediately.

"Take Samsung," Dhiraj chimed in.

I smiled. *"Who told you Micromax is poor in quality? And anyway, it's an Indian brand. If we don't support our own products, who will? The latest Micromax smartphones are great. Affordable, yet loaded with features that even Samsung or Sony phones offer at double the price."*

Dhiraj nodded. "True. My nephew has one. No complaints so far."

I opened the Micromax website and showed Hitesh a few models. After browsing through, he finally agreed to buy a Canvas phone. A small win for my personal mission—I always believed in promoting Indian products. Everything I used, from toothpaste to my bike and clothes, was Indian-made. It was my little rebellion against the global economic downturn.

While we were still talking, my phone buzzed. A message from Soumya.

"Thank you 100 times for making my day so beautiful. And guess what? Mumma gave me permission to learn bike riding from you... but only early mornings. So don't you dare sleep after 5 AM, or I'll kill you ? ? ?"

Her smilies lit up the message—and my heart.

Hitesh noticed the smile on my face. *"What happened, Mrinal? Blushing, are we?"*

I laughed, brushing it off. "Just a joke Soumya sent."

He leaned in, more curious than ever. *"Mind if I ask something?"*

"Go ahead," I said.

"Is Soumya the reason you're not coming to Dubai?"

That question hit me hard. My heart skipped a beat. How did he know? Trying to stay calm, I replied, *"No! Why would you even think that? What makes you say that?"*

"Just asking," Hitesh said, shrugging. *"Didn't mean to offend."*

I forced a smile. "I didn't mind."

"Well, have you booked your Bangalore tickets yet?" he asked, changing the subject.

"I'll do it tomorrow. Planning to leave on the 6th of May."

With that, they got up to leave, and I was left with a smile that wouldn't fade.

The Next Morning – 5:50 AM

A call from Soumya jolted me awake. Thanks to our late-night chats, I had only managed a few hours of sleep. But the moment I realized she was coming to learn bike riding, the sleep vanished.

I picked up the call. *"Hello?"*

"You sleepyhead! I've been calling for thirty minutes! Get ready—I'm on my way."

Ten minutes later, I stood outside, locking my door, just as she arrived.

She wore a long pink T-shirt and black trousers, her hair loose and uncombed, yet she looked impossibly cute. Brushing her hair aside, she reached out for the keys.

She kicked the bike—once, twice, six times—but it wouldn't start.

"I got this, don't laugh!" she warned, but finally looked at me for help.

Laughing, I said, "You forgot to turn on the ignition."

"What?"

"You just unlocked the handlebar. Let me show you," I said, twisting the key further. *"Now try."*

This time, the engine roared to life with a single kick. She moved a few meters, but the engine stalled again. I explained the clutch and throttle more patiently.

Soon enough, she was confidently riding in first and second gear. I joined her on the back seat for a while, guiding her through the controls. Once we reached a traffic-free road, I insisted she ride solo.

She hesitated, but I promised to run alongside. Her confidence grew with each loop. Two hours later, she was handling the bike like a pro.

Before heading back, she asked if I'd take her on a ride. I couldn't say no. She hopped on the back, and I sped along the national highway. The wind on our faces, her laughter ringing in my ears—it was pure joy.

After a while, I stopped the bike. **"Your turn now,"** I said.

"Nooo!" she protested, but relented when I insisted. This time, she was the one riding us back—her first time on the highway. Trucks and buses roared past, but she managed well.

Locals stared. It wasn't common to see a girl confidently riding a bike with a boy on the back.

She giggled, *"Everyone must be thinking I'm eloping with you! What if the police start chasing us?"*

We both laughed.

I asked her to stop for a moment. She pulled over.

"What's wrong?" she asked.

I pulled out my phone. *"Smile!"*

She stuck out her tongue instead, making a funny face that only made her look cuter. I took four photos, capturing her like this—joyful, wild, and free.

We reached home around 9:00 AM. Her mother looked worried, standing at the gate. Soumya waved it off and whispered to me, *"She's angry, but I don't care."*

Then she looked me in the eyes and said, *"Thank you for everything."*

She was happy. And me? I was the happiest man on Earth in that moment.

Thank you, Soumya. For your time. Your trust. And this unforgettable morning.

CHAPTER TWENTY-THREE

THE PROMISE

It was almost 11:00 AM when she came to me. Her steps were hesitant, eyes heavy—not from lack of sleep, but from the weight of disappointment.

"Did you see my JEE result?" she asked quietly.

"I did," I replied gently.

She didn't need to say more. Her face said it all.

"Papa and Mumma... both are really sad. I scored just 32. Only 32. I've ruined my career... and my life."

Tears brimmed in her eyes, but none had fallen yet. She was holding on, trying to stay composed.

I got up, walked over to her. *"Soumya... nothing is ruined. Not yet. You have a whole year ahead of you. We'll work harder this time—together. And next year, I promise, you'll shine. You'll rock. I know you."*

She looked up at me, those eyes searching for even a flicker of hope. *"Do you really believe I can do better next year?"*

I held her gaze, calm and steady. *"I don't just believe—I trust you. And I promise you this: you will get a good rank. But you must follow everything I say."*

A slight pause. Then she nodded, slowly, with resolve. *"I'm ready. I'll do whatever you say. I'm surrendering myself to you—literally. Just... get me a seat in IIT. I can't see Papa like this. I just can't."*

Her voice trembled on the edge of breaking. She wasn't crying, but the storm within her was loud.

To ease the tension, I smiled. *"But hey... I need something in return."*

Her brows lifted. "What?"

"A grand party at Mayfair once you get selected. And you will get selected."

A flicker of a smile appeared. *"I'm not promising Mayfair,"* she said, her *voice steadier now. "But I will give a party. That's a promise."*

The determination in her voice was back. That spark I knew and believed in had begun to glow again.

"When are you leaving for Bangalore?" I asked.

"I don't know exactly. But the tour will take about fifteen days, I think." Her tone was still unsure, distracted.

"Alright, go and enjoy the tour. After you're back, we'll start preparing to conquer next year. Deal?"

"Deal." She nodded, trying to hold a small smile.

"And what's the plan in Bangalore, anyway?" I teased. *"After all, I'll be there too..."*

"Arrey, first meet me there, then we'll talk about plans!" she said with a laugh that finally felt genuine.

I smiled. *"Now I have no doubt we'll meet there. Just keep your phone on and charged—no excuses."*

"Okay, okay. I'll keep it charged!" she said, raising her hands in mock surrender.

"I have to go now—so much packing left," she added, stepping toward the door.

"Take care. And don't forget—this is just the beginning."

"Bye," she said softly, and with a lingering glance, she left the room.

CHAPTER TWENTY-FOUR

THE WEIGHT OF COMPARISON

It was 7:40 in the evening when my phone rang. Her name flashed on the screen—Soumya.

"Hello?" Her voice was low, flat... almost broken.

"Soumya... are you okay?" I asked, a sinking feeling already settling in my chest. Something wasn't right.

"Hmmm," she murmured, and that one sound carried the weight of her entire world.

"Tell me what happened," I urged gently. *"I know you're upset."*

There was silence for a moment, then she began in her typical way—explaining the answer to a simple question with a trail of details.

"Do you know Jyoti? She was my classmate... She used to ask me lots of questions, always came to me for help with studies. We did our homework together at the hostel. She wasn't really good at academics."

Her voice cracked a little, just enough for me to feel the hurt behind it.

"She qualified for JEE Advanced."

I paused. That wasn't something I hadn't expected, but I could feel the storm that had begun brewing in her. Comparison was cruel—and personal.

"So what? Maybe she got lucky," I said lightly, though a harsher truth lingered unspoken in my head. If you'd studied half as much as you claimed to, and chatted less with Ansh... maybe you'd be the one qualifying today. But this wasn't the time for truth. This was the time for support.

"It's not just luck. I'm not saying that," she said quickly. *"I'm sure she studied hard. But I don't know what happened to me in those last 3–4 months before the exam. I just... stopped studying."*

Her voice trembled. The cracks widened. She was holding herself together, but barely.

"Babu, listen to me," I said softly. *"We still have eight to nine months. We'll shock everyone next year. I promise."*

She sighed. *"Whenever someone on Facebook asks my marks, I just log out. I don't even respond."*

"Pagal," I said, trying to sound playful, *"whenever someone asks now, just tell them you qualified for Advanced. Why give anyone the pleasure of seeing you feel low?"*

A surprised giggle escaped her lips. *"Hehehehehe... that's a good idea."*

"And next year," I continued, *"when you get 300-plus, just tell them you aimed for only the top IIT, so you dropped. Let them figure it out."*

That made her smile more. But then her voice turned quiet again, serious. *"You'll help me get a good rank next year... right?"*

"No," I said gently. *"You will get the rank. I'll be there with you, every step. But you'll do the work. All I ask is your 100% dedication. Nothing else."*

"I'll give it. I promise," she said, firm and clear.

"Then IIT is yours. That's my promise," I said.

There was a pause. Then she sighed again, softer this time. *"I don't even want to go to Bangalore now. But the tickets are booked... and no one from my family will be home. So I have to go."*

"Alright then. Full masti in Bangalore—after that, full tapasya in Bhubaneswar," I joked.

"Yes, okay." Her voice had lifted again, lighter now, warmed by hope.

"Go have dinner now," she said after a pause. *"We'll talk again after that."*

"Okay. Bye."

"Bye."

The line disconnected, but her voice lingered with me—wounded, but healing.

CHAPTER TWENTY-FIVE

SHADOWS OF DOUBT AND LIGHT

May 5, 2014 – Bhubaneswar Airport

We stood at the departure gate, the three of us wrapped in a long, quiet embrace. Hitesh and Dhiraj were all set for their first international business trip, and it showed in their eyes—excitement, nervous anticipation, and that unmistakable glint of ambition. Even Dr. Patra had taken time out to come to the airport. He stood by like a proud father, his eyes misty, his smile constant. His students were taking flight—literally—and somewhere deep inside, he knew they were destined for something big.

He wished them all the best, and I added my own reminder: ***"Stay in touch... Skype, WhatsApp, whatever it takes."***

I watched their plane disappear into the clouded Bhubaneswar sky — two of my closest friends, off to Dubai on our first international business trip. I should have been on that flight. Every logical part of me knew it. **But logic had stopped driving my decisions the moment Soumya entered my life.**

Dr. Patra looked at me during the drive home, his voice cautious but knowing. "Why aren't you going with them? This is your company, your idea... What could be more important?"

I gave him a rehearsed excuse about logistics and delegation. But the truth was buried under layers I couldn't peel in front of him — or anyone.

When we reached home, the silence hit harder than expected. I didn't just feel left out — I felt abandoned. Everyone had somewhere to be, something exciting to chase. And I was here, chasing a ghost through phone signals.

I checked my phone. No messages. No missed calls. Just blankness. For two hours, nothing from Soumya.

I called.

Busy.

Waited ten minutes.

Called again.

Still busy.

Called a third time.

This time she answered — just to say: *"I'll talk to you later, bye."*

She didn't say it rudely. But it wasn't lovingly either. It was the kind of tone you use when you have more important people on the other line. And it hit me hard.

For a moment, an ugly thought twisted inside me — was it Ansh again? Had I misread everything between us? I hated myself for even thinking that way. But when you care too deeply, logic fades. All that's left is your worst fear on repeat.

I sat on my bed, phone in hand, still and silent. Then, without warning, the tears came.

I had given up a major moment in my career — not because she asked me to, but because I wanted to be available for her. And now, in the moment I needed someone most, she was too busy.

Not angry. Just... busy.

The irony tasted like metal.

Hours Later, 5:00 PM

My phone rang. Her name flashed across the screen.

"Good morninggggg!" Her voice was cheerful, maybe even playful.

But I wasn't in the mood to play.

"Hmm," I said flatly.

"What's wrong with you? If you don't want to talk, just say so. Bye."

"Bye."

I wanted to scream Don't go, tell her how I'd waited all day. But instead, I let the silence win again.

A while later, she called again — this time, furious.

"You're so cheap! You hacked my Facebook just because I didn't talk to you?"

My breath stopped. What?

She didn't ask. She accused. Not, **"Did you do this?"** But, **"I know you did."**

She thought I'd hacked her account — posted her private pictures. The betrayal in her voice was louder than her words.

I swallowed my disbelief and tried to steady my voice. *"What happened exactly?"*

"I'm serious. If you don't return my password right now, you'll regret it."

I hung up. Not out of anger — out of heartbreak.

How did we go from 3 AM confessions and laughter to this?

I opened Facebook. Her wall was filled with her personal photos — embarrassing ones, meant only for her or close friends. Someone had clearly hacked her account. But not me.

I called her again.

"Soumya, I swear, I didn't do this. I can help fix it, but you have to trust me."

Her voice softened. *"Okay. Please... just recover it or deactivate it."*

Within an hour, I had her account back. Reset passwords. Added security. She hovered nearby, quiet now.

"You recovered it so fast... Are you sure you didn't do it?"

I forced a laugh. *"Knowing how to break a lock doesn't mean I steal."*

She nodded slowly. *"Can you make it more secure?"*

"Give me three trusted contacts."

"Okay. You, my mumma, and... Anushka."

It hit me then — she still trusted me more than anyone, except her parents. Even in anger, even in chaos. And maybe that's what hurt the most — that this bond could still be so fragile.

"I trust you like I trust my papa," she said, watching me type.

"Then why did you accuse me?" I asked.

"Because when I'm angry, or scared, or happy — you're the only person I feel I can shout at without breaking the bond."

And in that second, I knew. She wasn't angry at me. She was terrified of losing something — maybe herself, maybe trust, maybe just stability.

So was I.

We sat in silence for a moment, not quite healed, but not broken either.

"Packing done for Bangalore?" I asked.

"Yes! Already planned what to do."

"Oh yeah? What are we doing?"

She grinned. **"Bahut sari masti, pagalpanthi, movies and shopping!"** ("Tons of masti, madness, movies, and shopping!")

I smiled back.

And just like that, she was my Soumya again.

It was 2:00 AM. Just as I was about to fall asleep, my phone screen lit up. It was a message from Soumya.

"Sleep early, okay? I'll wake you up in the morning before I leave for Bangalore. Good night!"

So, she was finally free—probably done talking with Ansh. I replied simply, *"Ok... good night."*

But then came another message, ***How rude!! Can't you talk for 5 minutes? So busy??**"*

Oh Soumya... why don't you ever understand? Every second of my life revolves around you. It's you who drifts away, and yet you come back accusing me of neglect. I replied, *"Sorry, I thought you were going to bed. We can talk all night if you want."*

"May I call?" she asked.

"Yes," I said without hesitation.

She called.

"Hello," I answered.

"Have you packed everything?" she asked.

"Not yet. Just a few clothes and accessories left. Should take thirty minutes. When do I get to see you in Bangalore?"

"My parents' meditation starts early—5:00 AM on May 8th. Anytime after that."

"Okay, I'll come to take you."

"Okay... kitna maza aayega na?"

("Okay... it's gonna be so much fun, isn't it?")

"Yes... =D"

"Now go to bed. Sleep. Good night. Bye."

"Good night... bye."

She hung up. I was smiling. That small conversation meant everything to me. She had called. She wanted to meet. Plans were being made. I couldn't sleep. I kept replaying her words in my mind.

At 6:30 AM, I woke up as promised. I checked my phone—there was a message:

"Sorry, I couldn't come. Our train was at 5:20 AM. See you in Bangalore. Bye... take care."

Wait... didn't she say 8:00 AM?

I typed immediately: *"I woke up at 6:30 AM to say goodbye... and you left without seeing me. ☹ I miss you. Bye, happy journey."*

Within 30 seconds she replied:

"Awwww... missing me!! Don't be sad... we'll meet in just two days! Come safely. Bye."

I read that reply over and over again. Her words had a warmth that erased my disappointment. Especially those lines—"Awwww... missing me!!"

My train was at 10:50 PM. I had the day to myself and a bit of shopping to do. I was still sleepy, so I decided to nap for an hour.

Thirty minutes later, another message buzzed in:

"Please, listen to this song—'Ajanabi mujhko itna bata, mera dil kyun pareshan hai...' Message me after listening. Bye."

(*"Please listen to this song—'Stranger, just tell me this... why is my heart so restless?' Message me after you've heard it. Bye."*)

It was her thing—sending songs that captured what she felt but couldn't say outright. Time never mattered. Even at 2:00 AM, she would send me music.

I listened. A melancholic, old melody. I replied: "It's old but beautiful."

Her message came instantly:

"Pagal ho ap!!("You're such a mad one!!") *I was talking about the lyrics, not the music. Tell me about the lyrics."*

Still half-asleep, I fumbled: *"Lyrics were also good... but what are you trying to say?"*

"This song fits you. You were a stranger once. Now, whenever I'm upset or disappointed, I turn to you. You make me feel better."

"Pagal... you're going to Bangalore and still thinking about me?"

"Aur nahi to kya? Mazak chal raha hai kya??" She replied with her signature phrase.

("Duh! Do I look like I'm kidding??" she replied with her classic line.)

"Hehehehe... see you day after tomorrow. Bye."

By 9:00 AM, I had a mild headache from the broken sleep. I lay down again.

My phone rang. It was Hitesh.

"Hello, where are you?" I asked.

"We reached the client's place. Bro... he's really rich. If we nail this, we might land more deals."

"Of course we will! We always do. Dhiraj nervous?"

"A little. The client wants to show his entire business first—then we prepare a presentation for his board. If they approve, we sign."

"Hmm. So it'll take a week at least. That's good—I'll be back from Bangalore by then."

"Cool. Talk later—ISD bills!"

"Haha... sure. All the best."

He hung up.

And with him, my doubt returned.

Why was I going to Bangalore?

I wasn't her boyfriend. She didn't love me. She loved Ansh. Then why?

Because I loved her company. No, I needed her company. It made me feel whole.

Loving her was like loving a temple. You go for peace—not for the temple to love you back.

That's how I convinced myself.

11:10 PM. I boarded my train and messaged her that I'd reach around 4:00 AM two days later. No reply. Probably no signal. I turned off my phone and rested.

Morning. The train staff woke me up with tea. I turned on my phone—11 missed calls. All from Soumya.

I called immediately.

No answer.

Then a message: **"Don't call, I'll call you later. Bye."**

I replied: ***"When urgent: 1 missed call. If you miss me but can't call: 2 missed calls. No balance to talk: 3 missed calls. If parents watching: no call."***

Two missed calls came instantly. My Soumya missed me but couldn't talk. My heart smiled.

I messaged: ***"I miss you too... can't wait to see you in Bangalore. One missed call if you read this but can't reply."***

One missed call came. That was our code—our language when words weren't possible.

I had breakfast and started reading a novel.

A line struck me:

"A girl, no matter how many times she denies it, will always remember every detail, every moment, every memory you gave her."

Rubbish. It's not just girls. I could recall every word Soumya ever said. Every moment, etched in me.

Was I in love?

Was there even a point in going?
She loved Ansh. Why did she want me in Bangalore?
Only time would answer.
9:00 PM. Soumya messaged:
"Reached Bangalore. In cab to Ashram."
I replied: "Wait for me... I'll be there in 8 hours."
My journey wasn't just through cities or miles.
It was toward answers, clarity... and maybe closure.

CHAPTER TWENTY-SIX

BANGALORE ARRIVAL

The weather in Bangalore deserves all the praise. Bhubaneswar was scorching in May, but Bangalore's climate was surprisingly pleasant. Friends had often told me that Bangalore stays comfortable almost year-round—and they were right.

My train was just an hour late. This was my first time in Bangalore, and I had no idea where to go from the station. So I turned to Google for help and found a hotel about 7 kilometers from the Art of Living International Centre. I called and luckily got the last available room—a double bed. I booked it immediately and took a cab.

It was 5:30 AM when I texted Soumya: *"Just reached. On the way to the hotel now."*
No reply.

After checking in, I tried calling her. But an automated voice said her incoming services weren't available. That's when I realized she probably ran out of balance. I paused for a moment—how did her balance finish after just a few messages?

Then it hit me. She must've called Ansh after arriving in Bangalore. It made sense.

Still, I had to talk to her. I quickly recharged her number with ₹50 and called again.

She picked up.
Soumya: "Where are you? Did you recharge my account?"
Me: "Yes. I had to talk to you, and your incoming calls weren't working. Where are your parents?"
Soumya: "They're in meditation. Started early. Come soon, I'm bored!"
Me: "Wow, okay. I'm staying at a hotel near the ashram."
Soumya: "WHAT? Where??!! I'm coming over—send me the address."

Me: "No, I'll come get you. This city's new for you too. Wait 30 minutes."

Soumya: "Nothing will happen! I'll take an auto. Just send me the address."

Me: "Soumya, please don't be stubborn. It's not safe for you to come alone. Try to understand."

Soumya: "Either send the address or stop talking. Bye."

Sigh. I hung up and sent the address, asking her to stay on the call while traveling. I was really worried about her.

Then I went for a shower. Ten minutes later, I came out to five missed calls from her.

I called back immediately.

Me: "Hello? Where are you?"

Soumya: "Where were you?! Not answering my calls!" Her mock anger was obvious.

Me: "Sorry! Was in the washroom."

Soumya: "Okay, okay... I forgive you."

Me: "Where are you now?"

Soumya: "In the auto. Reaching in 10 minutes."

Me: "Call me once you're here."

Soumya: "Why? What's the problem with talking now?"

Me: "Pagal, I just got out of the shower... still in a towel!"

Soumya (laughing): "Hehehehe... Why not just say you're nangu pangu?"

Me: "Are you mad? What will the auto driver think hearing this?"

Soumya: "Mekko pagal bola! Bye! Mekko baat nahi karni!"

("You called me crazy? Hmph! Bye! I'm not talking to you anymore!")

Me: "Who said that? I meant the auto driver!"

Soumya: "Ohhh... then I'll keep talking." She said it in a cute voice.

I'd once read: "When a girl feels truly comfortable with you, she becomes a child again." Soumya was the perfect example. Her silly, spontaneous behavior always made me smile—even in my loneliest moments.

Eventually, I convinced her to hang up so I could get ready and meet her downstairs.

As soon as I combed my hair, her message popped up:

"Hum aa gaye hain, swagat nahi karoge mera? :D"

("I've arrived... won't you give me a grand welcome? :D")

I smiled.

I walked down from my room. She was waiting near the reception—blue jeans, black t-shirt, curly hair cascading like a dream. She looked... breathtaking. For a moment, I silently thanked God for creating something so perfect.

She stood up, catching me staring.

Soumya: "Is this the first time you're seeing me or have you just turned extra flirty in Bangalore?"

She grinned mischievously. I knew she was aware of how beautiful she looked.

Me: "If you could see yourself through my eyes... you'd probably blush, swoon, and then file a complaint for excessive compliments."

Soumya: "Oh, so you brought me here to flirt, huh? Can't trust you when no one's around!"

She grinned, eyes twinkling.

Me: "Okay then, stay here. I'll come back in 10 minutes."

Soumya: "No, I'm coming with you."

Me: "Fine."

When she saw the room:

Soumya: "Wow, what a room! And two beds... one's mine, right? :P"

Me: "Pagal, this was the only room available. So I booked it."

Soumya: "Oh, so you don't want to admit you booked a double bed just for me?"

She was in full-on crazy mode, and I loved every bit of it.

Me: "Where to now? Movie, mall, park, temple—options galore."

Soumya: "Let's go to a temple first. Prayers, prasad, peace."

Me: "Good idea. You're so intelligent."

Soumya: "Shut up!"

Me: "Okay, you're not intelligent. Happy now?"

Soumya (dramatically): "Mummaaaa... main kya karu is insaan ka?!"

(Soumya (dramatically): "Moooom! What do I even do with this guy?!")

Me: "Don't disturb Mumma. She's meditating."

She asked: "Which mall even opens at 8:00 AM?"

Me: "None."

Soumya: "Then plan after two hours. For now, feed me."

I pulled out a food packet from my bag. She snatched it.

Soumya: "Awwww! For me na? Thank you!"

She was the kind of girl who found joy in the smallest things—and I adored that.

She sighed: "If only you'd brought your bike, we could roam around the city!"

Me: "We can rent one!"

Her face lit up. We searched online, found a rental service, and within an hour, we had a Pulsar 150cc.

Now came her tiny wish: she wanted to drive. She'd only practiced riding for two days, but I agreed—on traffic-free roads only.

We fueled up and set off. I turned off my phone to conserve battery—for maps, just in case.

As I started the bike, she leaned toward me and said softly:

Soumya: "I'll never forget this. I feel like I'm not the same scared Soumya anymore. I feel brave. Like I can take on the world. Thank you for this feeling."

Me: "Wo sab to thik hai... but do you have any idea where we're going?"

Soumya: "How would I know? I'm a girl! This isn't my department. Don't stress my brain! Let me just enjoy this ride."

I smiled.

Bangalore's roads were smooth, but traffic in the city was chaotic. I opted for an elevated expressway. After a while, she asked:

Soumya: "Where are we going?"

Me: "Don't stress your brain—it's not your department!"

Soumya: "Shut up! Tell me."

Me: "First decide—should I shut up or speak up?"

Soumya: "Please na... tell me."

Me: "Keep riding straight for 10 more kilometers. Surprise ahead."

Soumya: "A surprise? What surprise??"

Me: "Wait and see."

The roads were almost empty now.

Soumya: "Can I drive?"

Me: "Of course. Let's switch."

She took the handlebars, nervous but excited. I encouraged her.

She started the bike smoothly.

Me: "You're driving like a pro!"

Soumya: "Talent!"

I laughed. I had hoped she'd say *"because of you."* But I knew she meant it.

Soumya: "So where are we going, finally?"

Me: "No spoilers. Just drive 10 more kilometers."

Soumya: "Are you planning to kidnap me?"

Me: "You're the one driving! Technically, you've kidnapped me."

"Oh God... what kind of man are you? A teenage girl kidnapped you! What face will you show the world now? Such shame!" she teased with mock seriousness, rolling her eyes dramatically.

Soumya never lost an argument—mostly because she had no intention of letting one end. And we? We thrived in this madness. Our nonsense battles could go on for hours and never reached any real conclusion—except that we secretly loved every minute of it.

Suddenly, she squealed in delight, pointing ahead. *"Wonderla! Are we really going to Wonderla?!"*

"How did you guess that?" I looked at her, genuinely surprised.

She smirked. *"Don't you know? Soumya is a genius."*

"Oh, please. It's only because you hang out with me. You're just catching my brilliance by association!" I joked.

"Thanks! So you do admit I'm a genius—whatever the reason!" She shot back, victorious as always.

"Okay okay, genius girl... BRAKES—FAST!" I shouted suddenly. She was about to bump into a car at the traffic light. I quickly reached out, taking control of the bike.

She looked a bit shaken.

"You alright?" I asked gently.

"Hmm... yeah."

"You were doing great, really. Just need a little more practice. You're almost there," I said, trying to reassure her.

"Hmm..." she murmured, calming down a bit.

I nudged her, *"Okay, back to the important stuff—how did you really guess we're going to Wonderla?"*

"Told you—it's my superpower!" she declared, regaining her playful spark.

Twenty minutes later, we were standing at the gate of Wonderla. We took a few goofy selfies, bought our tickets, and walked in like kids breaking into a candy store.

Wonderla—Bangalore's famous amusement park. Rides, water slides, rollercoasters, snacks, and chaos. My plan? Lunch somewhere inside, then lose ourselves in wave pools and loop-the-loops. I'd memorized the whole route on Google Maps earlier. I wanted this day to be one she'd never forget.

"So, oh brilliant one," I asked, *"which ride do we start with?"*

"Oh, am I a ride-specialist now? Duffer!"

"I thought you were a genius!" I teased.

"Shut up! Let's explore and see what we like." Her eyes sparkled.

"Wonder Splash?" I pointed toward a board.

"What's that?"

"Some water ride—we'll probably get soaked."

"So what? Wet clothes dry. Let's gooo!" she shouted, practically skipping. "And thanks... this surprise is amazing."

The Wonder Splash was a boat ride that blasted through water at high speed. She sat beside me and—whether out of excitement or just instinct—grabbed my hand tightly as the raft surged forward. With every twist and splash, she held me tighter. And in that moment, soaked and screaming, I felt more alive than I had in years.

Next up was the "Banded Kraits"—a giant water slide in a tandem raft. We flew down dark tunnels, splashing into shallow pools with laughter that echoed like music. And yes, she held on to me again.

We were drenched and starving. Lunch was next—a cozy eatery where we laughed about our rides and made fun of each other's expressions in the pictures.

Post-lunch? The Dungeon Ride. Spooky, supposedly. But we turned it into a comedy show, mocking every jump-scare like we were stand-up comics.

By then, it was 4:00 PM. She wanted to try the Rain Disco, but I reminded her we'd have to travel back wet. So we opted instead for the 3D Max show—an absolute hit. She was amazed. Her eyes sparkled like a kid on Christmas morning.

By 6:00 PM, we started our journey back, inching through Bangalore's infamous traffic. It took over two hours.

At 8:30 PM, we had dinner together at my hotel. I offered to drop her back to the Ashram.

She pouted adorably, *"Why?"*

"So you can rest. We'll head somewhere new tomorrow."

"But I don't want to leave..." she whispered.

"I don't want you to either," I admitted. "But the hotel doesn't have any spare rooms."

"Do you really want me to go?" She gave me a suspicious look.

"I never want you to go. But... for your safety..."

"Stop being diplomatic. Yes or no?"

"No!"

"Stupid! Then let's talk to the manager."

Turns out a room would be available—but only after 2:00 AM.

"No problem," she beamed. "I'll wait in your room. We never sleep before 3:00 anyway!"

I wasn't sure if I should be thrilled or terrified. My heart sang, but my mind whispered warnings. This wasn't guilt—it was fear. Fear of crossing some invisible line.

By 10:00 PM, we were in my room. She sat next to me, flipping through the day's photos, giggling at her own silly expressions. I noticed something odd—no calls from Ansh all day. And strangely, that made me happy.

As she scrolled, my phone pinged. A message from Hitesh.

"Come online on Skype."

"Must be important," I told Soumya.

She handed me the laptop. *"Go ahead. I'll finish these later."*

I connected, propping the laptop on the table, my legs hanging off the bed. As I talked with Hitesh, she quietly laid her head in my lap and started playing a game on her phone.

I didn't want the call to end. I needed it to. My whole body was hyper-aware of her touch.

Hitesh: "The client's impressed. Wants us at tomorrow's partner meeting. Might even propose a second project."

Me: "That's huge! Did he say anything specific?"

Hitesh: "Not yet. But get your visa ready. We might need you soon."

Me: "I'll be there. Count on it."

We wrapped up after 35 minutes. When I looked down, Soumya was fast asleep on my lap.

If I moved, I'd wake her. So I didn't. I sat there, motionless, just staring at her.

Her face was pure peace. In that moment, I silently compared her to every actress, every magazine model I'd ever seen.

None of them came close.

She wasn't just beautiful—**she was mine**. At least in this one fleeting moment.

Thirty minutes passed. My legs were killing me. To distract myself, I started browsing places we could visit the next day. Not malls. Not typical tourist spots.

I remembered something she'd once said—how she dreamed of helping underprivileged girls. Not for fame. Not for money. Just... because it made her happy.

So I found a place. A surprise. A visit that would touch her heart. I noted the address and route.

As I finalized the plan, she stirred.

"Good morning!" she said, eyes still closed.

"You're awake?"

"Nope. Sleep-talking," she giggled. *"What time is it?"*

"11:23 PM."

"Finished your chat with Hitesh Bhaiya?" she asked.

"Yes. Big things coming up for us."

"Yay! Make sure the deal gets signed. After all, you earn for me, right?"

My heart skipped. *"Of course. Who else?"*

"Paglu!" she laughed.

"You sleepy?" I asked, closing Facebook.

"Sleep? Now? You're kidding, right?" she grinned.

"Okay then, move a little. My legs are going numb."

"No way. Who's more important—your legs or me?" she pouted.

I smiled. *"You, obviously. Which is why I'm offering you an upgrade—a better pillow. One with background music."*

She sat up, laughing. *"Awwww... choo chweeeet!"*

She laying on bed keeping her head on my chest.

Soumya: *"You know, while I was a kid, I used to say mum mum to water and ghumun to cow. And when a cow comes to our gate, I used o give her newspapers to eat....but from a distance because I was scared from her that she may hurt me using her horns!!But still wanted to touch her!"*

Me: *"Hmmm"* I said.My eyes were closed, and I was listening her childhood stories with full attention.

"And whenever Papa or Mumma asks for the newspaper, I used to say ghumun ate them!! And at that time I used to think that cow eats news papers......!And you knew...., my mumma says that I never cried for anything while I was a kid!! Even not for milk or toys or anything...Mumma used to say that I was always happy....just give me a teddy bear, and leave me for hours!!!We start all dramma and everythng when we grew up and our sensory organs start feeling." I sensed a little pain in her voice.

"Hmm...when we start growing, we learn a lot about the world..about the people...we gradually learn to differentiate between 'own' people and 'other' people. Even we differentiate on different basis like 'rich' or 'poor' , 'pretty' or 'ugly', 'beneficial to us' or 'not beneficial to us' .And this process of

learning used to take our innocence. In the process of being a better human, we become just an 'actor' only..who acts differently with different people and even on different occasions.We become fake." I realized that I was talking like a philosopher.

"True!!" Soumya said.

"...And I know my Soumya is not fake...she is genuine...and I will not allow anyone to take her innocence. And I trust that she will be always a genuine person" I was serious while speaking.

*"Babu..."*She murmured

*"Hmmm...say".*It always felt good to hear babu for me from her.

"I hate you so much..." She said calmly.

"I know...you don't ".

*"I wanna cry".*Her voice was trembling.And that made me little worried. Was she sad even when she was in my arms?

I gently moved her head from my chest and sat up on the bed. She did the same, almost mechanically. Her eyes refused to meet mine, fixated instead on some invisible crack on the wall. Something was off. I leaned closer, cupped her face softly in my hands.

"Soumya... do you have a fever?" Her skin felt warmer than usual.

"I'm fine," she muttered and without warning, pulled me back into a hug—tight, needy.

"No, you're not. Please talk to me. Are you... are you feeling guilty about being here with me?" I whispered, holding her a little tighter now. Her body was burning up like someone running a temperature of 104°F.

"Please... don't say anything for the next ten minutes," she said, barely audible.

"Okay," I whispered back.

Five minutes passed. I gently raised her chin to meet her eyes. Her face had lost its color. She didn't need to say a word—her silence screamed louder. Her hands trembled against my back. I wiped the corner of her eyes, gently pulling her head back onto my chest.

"Are you okay, babu?" I asked in a voice barely above a whisper.

And then came the twist I wasn't expecting.

"Are all boys like you?" she asked, her voice dripping with mock annoyance. *"Are they all such... duffers?"*

Wait, what?

"What did I do now?" I blinked, confused.

She looked away. *"I just... need to go back to the ashram."*

"What? Why suddenly? Just wait a little. You'll get the room soon."

"It's not about the room. Or anything. I just..." Her sentence hung unfinished.

I noticed then—her breath was quick and uneven. Her fingers were clenched. The wrinkle on her nose bridge, that signature crease she had whenever she was nervous, was prominent now.

And then it hit me. She wasn't just warm—she was heating up. With emotions. With conflict. With... longing?

Suddenly, it happened. Without thinking, without processing—I felt the taste of her lips on mine. My mind blanked out. My senses dissolved. Her warmth, her nearness, the scent of her hair—it was all too much. I whispered into her ear, *"We can't... we shouldn't..."*

I gently pushed her back. I couldn't look her in the eye. My voice cracked. *"Soumya, I'm sorry. I didn't mean to... it wasn't intentional. I have no right over you, and yet I—"*

Before I could finish, she whispered, *"I can't resist you. I don't want to. I don't care what's right or wrong. I just... need this. I need you."*

Those words shattered every wall of self-control I had. Her vulnerability made me feel stronger, and yet, more helpless.

"Soumya, please..." I begged, though I wasn't even sure if I wanted her to stop.

My voice trembled. *"Oh God... hold me, please. I'll fall..."*

And she did.

Her lips found mine again. I cupped her face, feeling her hair between my fingers, and kissed her deeply—gently. There was a rhythm to it—unspoken, unstoppable. Her hunger mirrored mine. There was no turning back, no pretending this wasn't real.

But somehow, with every bit of willpower I had, I slowly pulled away again. My breath ragged. We sat there, silent, listening only to the sound of our own hearts crashing against our chests.

"Soumya," I finally said, eyes still downcast, *"Please forgive me for what almost happened. It wasn't planned. It wasn't right."*

She sat beside me, placed her head on my shoulder, and said softly, *"It wasn't your fault. Or mine. Sometimes, we just... feel too much. Maybe it's our age. Maybe the moment. But thank you—for stopping us. Please don't feel guilty, or I will too."*

Then she smiled. *"But... can I at least get one proper hug?"*

I grinned. *"Of course. Come here."*

She wrapped herself around me like home.

Then, in the most unexpected tone, she whispered:

"Marry me."

I blinked. **"What? Are you crazy? Ansh will kill us both!"**

I tugged her ear playfully.

She laughed. ***"I feel more connected to you than anyone else. I don't know if this is love or just madness, but I can't imagine being without you."***

Oh, Soumya. You just said everything I've felt for months. Except, for me, it was never about your body. It was always your soul I was in love with.

"I don't know what this is either," I said, brushing a strand of hair from her face. ***"But I feel like you're not separate from me. You're a piece of my soul, carved out, and allowed to grow somewhere else. And someday... I know I'll get that piece back."***

She raised her eyebrow, smirking. ***"Filmy dialogues! Which movie did you copy that from?"***

"Pagal! It's original. My own line," I chuckled.

"Well... it was too romantic."

"Thanks. I'll take that as a compliment."

She giggled.

"Paglu," she whispered.

7:05 AM – The Call

A soft vibration stirred me awake. Soumya's name flashed on my screen.

"Hello?" I answered, voice heavy with sleep.

"Mera babu uth gaya?" she asked, her voice laced with innocent sweetness.

("Has my baby woken up?" she asked, her voice wrapped in innocent sweetness.)

"Just woke up," I replied.

"I need my babu now."

"I need mine too," I mimicked her tone.

"Then come fast... I can't wait."

"Okay... coming." I smiled.

Within five minutes, I knocked on her door.

"Mera babu aa gaya?" she chimed, pulling me in. ***"Now I need a hug—on the bed."***

"Wow, good morning hugs?"

"Aur kya? Mazak samjha hai?" she pouted.

("What else? You thought I was joking?")

"Hehehe..."

"Come lie down... I don't want to get up. You know how lazy I am," she said, tugging me closer.

"Ohho, cuddling session?"

"You know everything... tharki insaan!" she teased.

("You know everything... you naughty creep!" (said playfully))

I finally understood why people say cuddling is the best part of a relationship. We lay there, limbs tangled, completely still. Time paused as we just... existed together. Her warmth, her breath on my neck, her fingers locked with mine—it felt like heaven. Or at least something I could trade my life for.

After 45 minutes, I whispered, *"Can I go now, babu?"*

"No," she gripped tighter.

"But it's almost 8."

"So what? I'm not letting you go—today or ever."

"But I really need to pee."

"Hehehe... that's your problem."

"Mera pagal babu."

"Paglu," she whispered back.

10:15 AM – Hotel

Somehow, every time I saw her, she looked newer—more radiant, more alive. Dressed in her favorite top and jeans, her uncombed hair only added to her charm. She smelled like fresh flowers, and her smile brightened everything around her.

"Stop staring at me or I'll complain," she teased.

"Oh really? To whom—your Papa?"

"No. Someone even scarier... he's very possessive and will beat you blue."

"Who?!"

"You, paglu."

"But I'm not possessive..."

"Hehehe... you are."

She hopped onto the bike. We headed to D'Mart, where I picked up chocolates, puzzles, crayons, and drawing books. She kept asking why—but I kept the surprise to myself.

We then arrived at our destination: a girls' orphanage.

"Wait... are you planning to adopt a child? Without marriage?!" she gasped.

"Yes. I've been thinking about it for a while," I joked.

"Suno, I'm not in the mood for your jokes. Tell me the truth."

"Relax. Spend some time here—you'll enjoy it, I promise."

She finally smiled. We got permission to meet the kids and distribute the gifts. There were around 100 girls, aged 6 to 13. Today was a holiday for them, and a few approached us curiously. Soumya immediately warmed up to them, helping with puzzles, organizing competitions, and making them laugh.

Watching her blend so seamlessly into their world filled me with pride.

She even tested their academic knowledge, but seeing how little they knew made her visibly sad. She whispered that she wished she could teach them every day, but we both knew that wasn't possible in Bangalore.

As we played, distributed chocolates, and had lunch with the kids, one little girl asked Soumya, *"Sister, I want to be beautiful like you. How?"*

Soumya blushed and said, *"You're already more beautiful than me. You don't need to be anyone else."*

That answer. That heart. That was my Soumya.

2:30 PM – Back at the Hotel

Tired but smiling, we returned to the hotel.

Soumya: *"So what's the plan for the rest of the day?"*

Me: *"I was thinking of shopping—I need to prep for Dubai."*

Soumya: *"Hmm. But first, take some rest."*

Me: *"Okay."*

Soumya: *"Also, I need to tell you something..."*

Me: *"Yes?"*

Soumya leaned close, brought her lips near my ear, and then—kissed my cheek.

"Hehehe... fooled you! Look at your face—you're blushing like a girl!"

I lunged to catch her, but she jumped on the bed, shielding herself with a pillow. I climbed after her and grabbed her from behind. She pushed me off balance, and I fell on the bed. She quickly sat on my belly, pinning my hands.

"Now tell me... what will you do to me?" she giggled.

I didn't respond. I used my legs to pull her closer, and before she could react, her face was in my hands. She didn't resist.

We kissed. Soft, slow, full of emotion. Then a little deeper. Passionate.

Soon, maybe out of exhaustion or emotional high, we drifted into sleep, wrapped in each other's arms.

7:40 PM – Waking Up

I woke up. She was still beside me, pretending to sleep.

"I know you're awake," I whispered in her ear. *"Get up, or I'll eat your ears."*

She smirked, eyes still closed.

I clicked a photo of her innocent smile, then mischievously took her finger and brought it near my nose.

"Stupid!" she yelped, pulling her hand back.

"Hehehe... how was that?"

"Dirty! Ruined the whole romance."

"So you weren't sleeping?"

"Now stop pretending."

"Okay, sorry. Hug?"

"No."

"Why?"

"Stock over."

"I have infinite hugs," I said, wrapping my arms around her.

"Leave me, gande insaan."

("Leave me, you dirty fellow!" (said in a teasing, flirty tone))

"I'm sorry," I said in a pitiful tone.

"Okay, okay... apology accepted."

"Hehehe..."

"Don't smile—hug me properly, duffer!"

"Pagal..."

It was 8:15 PM. We skipped shopping and went to a nearby restaurant instead.

Late Night Confessions & Quiet Cravings

It was now 10:45 PM.

Soumya was browsing through the day's photos on my laptop. When she paused on the picture of the little girl who'd asked, *"How can I look as beautiful as you?"*—I saw her blush.

"Everyone wants to look like Soumya, huh?" I teased.

"Hehehe... but only one person will ever look like me."

"Who?"

"Little Soumya," she said playfully.

"Wait... what do you mean?" I asked, surprised.

"Our daughter, paglu," she said, effortlessly.

That one word—our—threw me off. Did she mean me and her? Or her and Ansh? Should I be happy or heartbroken? Why did she always leave me in this sweet, unbearable confusion?

"But how are you so sure it'll be a daughter and not a son?" I asked with a wink.

"SHUT UP! I just know it'll be a daughter, and she'll look exactly like me! She'll be so mischievous, right?"

"No... she'll be cute—cuter than you."

"And she'll have these tiny fingers and legs... and hold my finger tight..."

"Hmm..." She was drifting into a dream.

"She'll stare at me with her sparkly little eyes and one day call me Mumma. I'll buy tiny frocks and dress her like a fairy..."

She looked like she could cry from happiness.

Then suddenly, a shadow passed over her face.

"I don't want a daughter," she said softly.

"What? But... why?" I asked, confused by her sudden change.

"I don't want her to suffer like I did. No daughter." Her eyes dimmed.

I understood. She hadn't forgotten what happened with her Mausajee. We men can never truly understand the fear, the daily humiliation, the hidden trauma girls endure—on streets, in malls, even in their own homes.

"But babu... we can raise her to be strong. Not a showpiece—but a fighter. Someone who protects not just herself, but other girls too."

"Hmm..." She seemed to come back to herself. *"And what did you say... our daughterrrrr?"* She dragged the words out, teasing me.

"No, I didn't!" I protested—though I had.

"Don't lie!"

"I'm sorry... I didn't mean to..."

"Pagalu..." she whispered.

That one word, that smile—it told me everything and nothing at once. Did she also imagine a life with me? Even while being committed to Ansh?

A New Morning

It was almost 1:00 AM when we finally slept in our own rooms.

The next thing I remember is waking up to her call. 7:00 AM. Not my usual hour—but I felt fresh.

"Let's go for a walk," she said.

Bangalore mornings in May are still a bit cool. And walking with the most beautiful girl in the world? That's more energizing than coffee.

"You always sit and work... you need this daily or you'll become unfit!" she scolded.

"I'll walk every day—on one condition."

"What now?"

"You have to come with me."

"Shutttt up!"

"Remember the last time we went for a walk together?"

"Hehehe... of course! I was learning to ride a bike and the tire got punctured! You forgot your wallet, and I had to pay. That was one of my favorite memories."

She took my hand—maybe unknowingly. Her hand was slightly cold.

We talked about everything—college, hostel stories, silly fights. I realized that walking with the one you love is far better than any long drive.

By 9:00 AM, after some hot breakfast, we returned to the hotel. Shopping day had begun.

Mantri Square Mall – A Day Out

By 11:00 AM, we were at Mantri Square—one of India's largest malls.

"Malls are made for couples like these," Soumya said, gazing at a cute western couple.

She held my hand almost the entire time.

She insisted I buy a purple shirt. *"When Soumya is around, she decides what you wear!"* she declared.

"And I'll pick something for you," I offered.

"No no! I can't. My mumma will ask too many questions."

"Then buy something unnoticeable—like a novel. You love reading."

"Hmm... good idea."

We spent over three hours shopping. She bought two novels from a young author. At first, she refused to let me pay—but eventually accepted them as a gift after my persistent coaxing.

Lunch followed, then a few more hours in the entertainment zone before heading back.

Back to the Hotel – Caring, Pizza & Playful Dessert

By 7:30 PM, my head was throbbing—maybe from the Bangalore traffic or skipping evening tea. I collapsed onto the bed. Just then, a message from Soumya:

"Do you have medicine for headache?"

I rushed to her room.

She looked tired too. I sat beside her, took her head onto my lap, and gently massaged her forehead.

After ten minutes, I asked, *"Feeling better?"*

She smiled, "Do you think I'll say yes and lose this massage? No way!"

"Hehehe... okay, but let me order pizza first."

"Stupid! Why are you taking care of me when you're tired too?"

"...Because I feel better when you feel okay."

"Paglu... now lie down. My turn."

"No no... I'm okay."

"SHUT UP! I'm a strong girl. Do as I say!"

Her gentle fingers worked magic. Fifteen minutes in, my headache vanished.

We shared a family-sized pizza, feeding each other, laughing like kids. They were my wonder moments.

Then I asked, *"Dessert?"*

"I have a plan," she grinned.

"What now?"

"Come closer, I'll whisper it..."

I moved in.

Smack.

She kissed my cheek. *"There! My dessert is done!"*

"But I haven't had mine," I said, pulling her close.

We kissed. We hugged.

<u>Sweet Uncertainty</u>

"Is it necessary to go to Dubai?" she asked.

"Yes. But I'll return soon, I promise."

"I won't stop you—I know your dreams. But... I'll miss you like hell."

"You won't miss me more than I'll miss you."

"Don't ever dare to forget me."

"I couldn't even if I tried. Missing you is like breathing—it'll only stop when I die."

"Awww... when did you start loving me this much?"

"I don't know."

I really didn't. What were we doing? What were we? She loved Ansh—but everything we shared felt so real. So right. So... confusing.

The Night That Didn't End

"Oh right—the novel!" I remembered.

"Oh yes!" she lit up.

We lay side by side, sharing a pillow, reading together through the night.

It was 7:14 AM when we finished.

We hadn't slept.

We were starving, so we walked to a nearby restaurant and devoured two Masala Dosas.

On the way back, Soumya teased, *"We didn't even brush our teeth!"*

By 9:00 AM, we collapsed into bed in our respective rooms.

The Goodbye

The next evening, Soumya's parents were finishing their course. I had to drop her off at the Ashram.

She was unusually quiet.

"Soumya... you okay?"

"Yes." Her voice was small.

I pulled her close. She leaned on my shoulder. It was wet. She was crying.

"No one can separate us," I whispered. *"I'll always be in touch. I promise."*

"I don't know why, but I'm scared," she whispered. *"You'll make new friends... get busy... forget me."*

"Soumya, yes—I may get new friends. I may be busy. But forgetting you? That's impossible. You're part of my soul. Even if I wanted to forget you, my soul wouldn't allow it."

"Awww... since when did you love me this much?" she smiled, wiping tears.

"I don't know..." I said.

But I was still wondering...

What were we?

It was around 4:30 PM when I reached at Sri Sri Ashram to drop Souma. While walking past the Ashram gates, we saw a familiar sight—a wrinkled old beggar, sitting beneath the same peepal tree as before.

Soumya stopped in her tracks and smiled.

"That's him!" she whispered dramatically, nudging my arm.

"Who?"

"Him! The baba [old man] I donated 100 bucks to the other day."

"Oh. Good."

She sighed. *"I'm totally broke today."*

"Want me to get you something?" I offered.

She shook her head quickly, lowering her voice. *"No! Mom and dad's meditation ends today. If they sense I took money from a guy... even an oxygen mask won't save me from their glares."*

I grinned. *"So what's the plan? Survive on fresh air and leftover blessings?"*

She turned to me, her eyes sparkling with mischief. *"Nope. Plan B."*

Before I could ask what that was, she walked straight toward the beggar with the confidence of a CEO about to close a deal.

"Namaste, baba! [Hello, old man!]" she said sweetly.

The beggar looked up, squinting at her.

"Yaad hai? [Do you remember?]" she asked. *"Do din pehle [Two days ago] I gave you Rs 100."*

His face lit up in recognition. *"Haan beti! Haan! Aap firse kuch dene ayi ho? [Yes, daughter! Yes! Have you come again to give something?]"*

I was already covering my mouth to stop myself from bursting out laughing.

She folded her hands innocently. *"Nahi baba... aaj lene aayi hoon. [No, old man... today I've come to take something.]"*

His face froze in confusion.

She leaned forward, lowering her voice like it was some national secret. *"Aapko yaad hai na... main ne aapko madad ki thi? Ab aapki baari hai. [You remember, right... I helped you? Now it's your turn.]"*

The poor guy looked puzzled. *"Ka... kya? [Wha... what?]"*

"Bas chhoti si madad chahiye, [Just a small help is needed,]" she smiled, *"Sirf dus hazaar rupaye. [Only ten thousand rupees.] Mujhe aapse udhaar chahiye. [I need a loan from you.]"*

He blinked, probably trying to reboot his system.

I lost it right there—laughing like an idiot, bending over on the footpath.

Soumya stood there straight-faced, like she was having a perfectly reasonable business exchange.

"Dekho baba, main udhaar le rahi hoon. Wapas bhi karungi. Aapka paisa safe hai. [Look old man, I'm taking a loan. I'll return it too. Your money is safe.]"

The beggar was still trying to process this divine plot twist.

Finally, Soumya broke into a grin.

"Chinta mat karo, baba. Aaj thoda mazaak kar liya. Aapki dua chahiye bas.

[Don't worry, old man. Just did a little mischief today. I only need your blessings.]"

She handed him another Rs 20 and bowed playfully.

As we walked away, I was still laughing, wiping tears from my eyes.

"You're mad," I said.

She winked. *"Pagal hoon. [I'm crazy.] But admit it—you were sad, and I made you laugh."*

I didn't reply.

I just looked at her, walking beside me like nothing happened, arms swaying, eyes gleaming under the Bangalore sun.

And in that moment...

I realized just how much joy one person could pack into such a tiny frame of madness.

When I returned to the hotel after dropping Soumya off. I was upset—deeply. I tried to distract myself, but the ache lingered like a shadow. As soon as I entered my room, I checked my phone.

There it was—a message from her:

"Miching yewww ☹"

A small smile formed on my face. I immediately replied:

"Missing you too, babu...feeling like seeing you again, right now."

Her response came instantly:

"Call!"

Without hesitation, I tapped her name and the call connected.

"Hello..." she said softly, her voice barely a whisper.

"Arey... are you okay?" I asked gently.

"Feeling strange... lonely... can you talk to me for a few minutes?"

"Why just a few minutes? I'll stay on the call until you fall asleep," I promised.

"When are you flying to Dubai?"

"Tomorrow morning, 10:30 AM. Emirates flight 565."

"And when will you reach?"

"Around 1 PM, local time."

"Always stay in touch—on WhatsApp or Facebook, okay?"

"Of course. You're overthinking. Everything will remain the same, Soumya... only we won't be physically present. But we'll always be in—"

Before I could finish, an automated voice interrupted:

"Your call is on hold, please wait..."

I assumed her grandfather was calling, so I waited. Five minutes passed. The call didn't resume. I hung up.

Fifteen minutes later, I called again—busy.

It didn't sit right with me. She never spoke to her grandparents for more than a few minutes. Who was she talking to now that she couldn't answer my call?

I tried again five minutes later. Still busy. When she finally picked up, she simply said she'd call me later.

And in that moment... I knew.

It had to be Ansh.

She had never ignored me like this for anyone else. I always knew she wasn't mine, but this hurt more than I had expected. Just a while ago, she was saying she missed me—was crying on the phone—and now she didn't even have a minute?

My heart sank. I felt a sudden downpour behind my eyes. Every moment we had spent together in the last few days started playing like a loop in my mind. I couldn't believe how weak I had become—how much her attention, or even her silence, now affected me.

To distract myself, I logged into Skype and saw Hitesh online. I told him I'd be landing in Dubai at 12:45 PM at Al Maktoum International Airport. He said he'd be there to receive me. We talked for a while, but even after signing out, I kept checking my phone... again and again.

It was now 1:40 AM. I was still awake, waiting for a goodnight message from her. I knew she wouldn't forget.

I was right.

At 1:41 AM, a message appeared:

"Gunnyt...take care."

Two minutes later, another one:

"If you're still not sleeping, listen to this song from the movie Zid... Tu Zaroori Sa Hai. After that, call me! Bye."

I opened YouTube and searched for the song.

Aisa laga mujhe pehli dafa, tanha main ho gayi yaara...
Hu pareshan si main, ab yeh kehne ke liye...
Tu zaroori sa hai mujhko, zinda rehne ke liye...

(It felt like, for the first time, I was truly alone, my love...

I'm restless now, just to say...

You've become essential to me—

Like breathing, to stay alive.)

The song—sung by Arijit Singh and Sunidhi Chauhan—was heartbreakingly beautiful. A melody so tender, it felt like it had been written just for us.

I called her after the song ended.

Me: "Hello?"

Soumya: "How was the song?"

Me: "Mind-blowing…"

Soumya: "And the lyrics?"

Me: "Too romantic…"

Soumya: "You know… this song fits me right now. You're necessary for me to stay alive. Tu zaroori sa hai mujhko, zinda rehne ke liye…"

Her words melted something inside me. I wasn't sure if she was serious or just being poetic. But one thing I knew with certainty—she was necessary for me to stay alive.

And then, like an idiot, I said it.

Me: "Hmm… and what about Ansh?"

Goddamnit. What had I done?

Her tone changed instantly.

Soumya: "What do you mean by Ansh? I love him. No one can replace him. He's my soulmate. Got it? I never expected your mentality to be this low. Don't call or message me again. Bye!"

She disconnected.

I sat there, stunned.

Just minutes ago, I was someone **"necessary to keep her alive."** Now she didn't want even my texts.

I didn't understand. What had I really done wrong? My heart clung to the hope that she was just emotional—overreacting—and maybe she would call back. Maybe she'd realize I didn't mean to hurt her.

To patch things up, I texted:

"I'm really sorry, Soumya. I know I made a big mistake, but I never meant to hurt you."

The message was delivered instantly. No reply.

Ten minutes passed. Still nothing.

I messaged again:

"Soumya… I'm leaving the country tomorrow. Will you really let me go like this?"

Still no reply.

One last time, I wrote:

"Ok, Soumya... you've made it clear how much I mean to you. Thanks. Bye. Take care."

I switched off my phone. But after ten minutes, I couldn't resist. I turned it back on, praying for a message.

Nothing.

I lay there, questions haunting me. How can someone change so quickly? Was anything real? Was I just her time-pass? Did she ever feel anything?

I had no answers.

It was almost 7:00 AM when I woke up. My head was heavy, and my heart even heavier, still aching from everything that happened last night. A part of me still clung to the hope that she would call or at least text to say goodbye.

I booked an Ola cab for the airport, scheduled for 8:00 AM. As the cab cruised through the quiet morning streets, my phone vibrated.

It was her.

For a moment, I hesitated. My first instinct was to ignore the call—to let her feel the same pain I had felt last night. But then, I realized it was always me who got hurt. She probably wasn't even thinking about me. Still, my foolish heart hoped.

I picked up.

Me: "Hello... I'm in a cab. Sorry, didn't feel the vibration earlier."

Soumya: "Okay... I wanted to see you before you left, but you ruined everything last night."

Me: "I'm sorry for that. I'll call you from the airport. The signal here is weak—can't hear you clearly. Bye for now."

I hung up.

No *"I'm sorry,"* no regret—just blame. And yet... I felt a strange comfort that she had at least called. What a fool I was.

At the airport, I tried calling her again. The line was busy. I gave up and went through the check-in process, immigration, and security, which took nearly 45 minutes. When I finally checked my phone, there was a message from her:

"Happy journey... ttyl. Bye ☺ "

To anyone else, it might have seemed polite. To me, it felt like a knife—cold, distant, final. I couldn't help but interpret it cynically:

"I'm busy with Ansh, I don't care where you're going. Maybe I'll talk to you if I feel like it."

I knew she wouldn't call. ISD rates were expensive, and even messages cost more. The only real hope was WhatsApp. But even that felt like a stretch.

I was flying far away—not just physically, but emotionally too. She was drifting. Or maybe... this was the real her all along.

As I boarded, the announcement instructed all passengers to switch off their mobile phones and fasten their seatbelts. I looked at my phone one last time, sighed, and powered it down.

CHAPTER TWENTY-SEVEN

BETWEEN DEALS AND DESIRES

Dubai is 90 minutes behind Indian Standard Time. I adjusted my watch accordingly, but the emotional clock inside me still ticked back home.

This was my first international trip, and I should've been excited. And I was... in some strange, hollow way. The plane landed at Terminal 3. The moment I stepped out, the warm, humid air of Dubai wrapped around me. It was unlike anything I had experienced before.

I wanted so badly to share that first impression with Soumya. But I knew—she wouldn't be waiting to hear it. So I just informed my family that I had landed safely.

After immigration checks and collecting my luggage, I found Hitesh and Dhiraj waiting outside. Their faces lit up when they saw me, which brought some comfort. I joined them and we walked toward the taxi stand.

"In Dubai, even Mercedes cars are used as taxis," Hitesh said with a grin.

Back in India, that would've been a symbol of luxury. Here, it was just another ride.

"So what's so special about Dubai?" I asked.

"It's a WOW place," Hitesh said enthusiastically. **"Fifty years ago, this was just desert. Now look at it—massive buildings, luxury, no taxes. It's unbelievable."**

He was right. If ever there was a model for extraordinary development, it was Dubai. Giant skyscrapers, stunning highways, malls dripping with extravagance—it all screamed success.

"And what about the client?" I asked, suddenly shifting gears. "Did the board finalize the project?"

He answered all my questions at once. And the news was good—our company was on track to become an official partner. We'd handle all their software and web needs. It was a big deal for us. Maybe a small milestone in the industry, but a huge one for our company.

We reached our accommodation in about two hours. It was in an area called Jumeirah, which Dhiraj told me means "beautiful" in Arabic. And it truly was—our new home for the next two or three months was gorgeous, located near the coast. There would be plenty of ways to unwind when off duty.

The apartment, provided by the client, was modest but well-furnished. Two bedrooms, a hall, two balconies—comfortable and cozy. One of the walls had a large poster with Arabic text. I had no idea what it said.

Hitesh told me to freshen up quickly—we had a client meeting after lunch.

After showering, I checked my phone.

Three Facebook messages from Soumya.

Soumya: Whr r u now??? :o :o

Soumya: All d best fr ur work... ☺

Soumya: bbye..tc

I smiled.

Despite everything... she had messaged.

Maybe she had a minute to spare between calls with **Ansh**. Maybe something reminded her of me. I didn't know. I didn't care.

I just replied:

Me: Thanx..bye..tc

I wanted to say more—so much more. I wanted to tell her about the weather, the airport, the excitement, the Mercedes taxis, everything. But something inside me held back.

Maybe pride.

Maybe pain.

Maybe fear that I'd get pulled back in, only to be hurt again.

After lunch, we left for the client meeting. The office was located in one of the glittering towers of Business Bay—an upscale commercial area in Dubai. The building itself was a marvel of glass and steel, towering like a monument to ambition.

We were a bit early, so we waited in the lounge. I was trying to appear calm, but inside I was nervous. This meeting could mark a turning point for our company—and for me, personally. A successful collaboration here would open international doors.

The client's team finally arrived, and we were called in. The room was professional, the atmosphere formal but welcoming. Our client, Mr. Kareem, greeted us with a warm smile and a firm handshake.

Hitesh and Dhiraj did most of the talking initially. I observed quietly, absorbing the tone and body language. When it was my turn to present the technical aspects of our proposal, I walked them through the architecture, scalability, and security protocols in detail.

To my relief, the response was positive. Mr. Kareem appreciated our clarity and depth, and he seemed genuinely impressed with the roadmap we had drawn up.

After about an hour, we wrapped up with handshakes and smiles.

"We'll be in touch very soon," Mr. Kareem said, and something about his tone made it sound more like a promise than a formality.

As we stepped out of the office building, the Dubai sun had begun to mellow into a golden glow. It felt like the city was applauding our small victory.

We decided to head back to the apartment to relax. In the cab, my mind drifted again—to her.

I pulled out my phone, half-hoping to see another message from Soumya. **Nothing.**

I opened our chat and stared at it for a few seconds, debating whether I should message her. Should I tell her how the meeting went? Should I share my happiness?

But no—I held myself back.

Something about her messages from earlier still lingered in my mind. They felt... distant. As if she were talking to someone she used to know, not someone who had just left her side a few hours ago. I didn't want to appear desperate. I didn't want to chase after someone who was slowly walking away.

By the time we reached our apartment, the fatigue of the day was starting to hit. I collapsed on the bed, staring at the ceiling. My thoughts were tangled—half about work, half about her.

Maybe more than half about her.

I wanted to let go. I really did. But some memories are sticky—clinging to your heart no matter how far you fly.

*

The meeting with the client had just concluded. He seemed genuinely delighted to see me—his warm handshake, enthusiastic tone, and affirming nods said it all. Most importantly, we signed the Memorandum of Understanding (MoU). Under this agreement, our company would handle all software and web development requirements for his global operations. We were now responsible for maintaining and managing the complete database of all his international offices.

It was one of our biggest milestones yet. Our startup was no longer just a small venture—it was becoming a recognized name, backed by a major international player.

Very soon, we were to begin work on a software system that would oversee and integrate his worldwide operations. He wanted every activity from each of his offices and shipping units to be tracked in real time. The system we were building wasn't just going to simplify his work—it was projected to save him millions of dollars annually.

As we stepped out of the towering office building, sunlight hit my face, but the real glow was inside me. My heart was racing with excitement. All I wanted in that moment was to share this victory—**with her.**

Without thinking, I pulled out my phone and dialed her number.

It rang once... twice... and then stopped. No answer.

I stared at the screen for a few seconds, the joy in my chest dimming just a little.

Her phone had rung. She wasn't busy. That could only mean one thing—she was likely with her parents. And that was reason enough for her to ignore me.

A familiar ache nudged my ribs. That quiet kind of hurt when you realize the person you want to celebrate with might not feel the same urgency. But I shook it off. I had a victory to hold on to—one that deserved to be celebrated, even if alone.

I scrolled through my contacts and called Dr. Patra instead.

Within three minutes, I had poured out everything—the new partnership, the successful pitch, the positive response. His voice sparkled with joy.

"I'm so proud of you," he said. *"This is a big milestone!"*

After hanging up, I glanced at my phone again—and smiled faintly.

Three Facebook messages. From her.

Soumya: Congratulations and lots of good wishes... ☺
Soumya: And one more thing... don't forget you're earning for me only. So work hard! I don't want any losses...
Soumya: Badly miss you ☹
Soumya: I'll message you from Kochi. We're about to catch the train. Bye, take care.

For a moment, I just stared at the screen, letting her words sink in. That mix of teasing, care, and that final—"badly miss you"—felt like rain after a drought. Bittersweet and unexpected.

Hitesh noticed the sudden lift in my expression.

"Arrey Mri... what happened? Why are you smiling out of nowhere?"

I quickly masked it.

"Nothing, man. Just a stupid joke on Facebook," I lied.

He shrugged and moved on. I stayed behind for a second longer, soaking in the strange warmth inside me.

I typed out a reply, my fingers speaking what my heart wanted her to hear:

Me: I miss you too... I really wished you were here, so I could celebrate this with you. I want to visit Dubai with you someday... to see the excitement on your face when I tell you everything. I'll send you photos... I just wish you could be part of this moment.
Me: Bye for now. Take care.

That should have been enough. But was it?

Maybe not. But I had to leave it at that.

We were in high spirits that evening. The deal had gone through, and that called for celebration. Dubai had plenty of options to explore, so I suggested a few places from Google—tourist spots, malls, cultural sights.

But Hitesh and Dhiraj exchanged glances and smirked.

"None of that," Hitesh grinned. "Dhiraj has a different kind of plan. He wants to drink."

I raised a brow. "And you?"

"I'm just the backup. Someone has to keep him company. And since you don't drink..." He laughed.

I joined in. "Fine. I'll come along—not to drink, but every drunkard needs a designated friend."

And so we set off. Our destination? A well-known place called MMI Dubai—part liquor store, part bar. As we walked in, sleek television screens flashed regulations and warnings. One of them caught my eye.

"You must present a liquor license along with your passport to purchase alcohol."

I couldn't help but laugh at their confused expressions.

"So, Dhiraj... do you have a liquor license?" I teased.

"What the hell is a liquor license?!" Hitesh exclaimed.

I explained: in Dubai, consuming alcohol without a license is a serious offense. Even taking liquor home requires proper documentation. Licenses are only given to residents—and processing takes at least a day.

Realizing the dead end, we laughed it off and settled for something we knew well: good Indian food. We had dinner and called it a night, the celebration still sweet, even without alcohol.

Next Morning

At 9:00 AM, I logged into Facebook.

No messages from Soumya.

She was online, though.

I stared at the screen, hesitant, then typed a quick "Hi" and sent it. Five minutes passed—nothing. She hadn't even seen it.

I sighed and logged out.

After breakfast, we headed to the client site. The next few days were meant for in-depth study of their operations. We needed to understand every detail to develop the software they wanted.

Despite the demanding schedule, I felt a kind of pride. India had truly made a name for itself in the software world. One of the Swedish engineers, struggling with broken English but eager to connect, spoke warmly of India's space success—Mangalyan was still a topic of admiration.

"India's first attempt... and still successful!" he beamed.

We couldn't help but feel a little taller in that moment.

Around 3:00 PM, we finally took a lunch break. I checked my phone.

There they were—several messages from Soumya, sent nearly two hours ago:

Soumya: Yaar such a killing place yaaaaar!!

Soumya: So beautiful I can't describe in words...

Soumya: We saw a houseboat—just like in the movies!

Soumya: Soooo romantic it was!

Soumya: R u thr??

A soft smile crept across my face.

She still shared her joys with me. Just like old times.

I replied:

Sorry, I was quite busy today. I'm here now...

She saw it instantly. And then came the reply:

Soumya: I'm in Kerala now... Munnar. Damn beautiful place.

Me: Yes, I've heard.

Soumya: It rains all the time here... still drizzling now.

Me: Ohh...

Soumya: It's freezing! Can you imagine—I'm under three blankets!

Soumya: I was just thinking... imagine if instead of Bangalore, we'd spent five days here.

Soumya: I seriously wish to visit Kerala with you again someday...

Me: Really??

Soumya: Hehehe... don't get too excited. I'm not planning my honeymoon with you, stupid!

Me: Arrey... I didn't mean it like that!

Soumya: Paglu.

Me: Hehehehe.

Soumya: And you know—we even rode a Shikara!

I smiled at my phone.

Me: Can we chat later tonight? Lunch just arrived, and I've got tons of work after that. I'll be free after 9:00 PM.

Soumya: Okey... sure. Bye.

I didn't want to end that conversation. Never did. But today, I had no choice.

Still... I was happy. Deeply happy.

She still thought of me.

Still wanted to share her little moments.

Still found joy in letting me into her world.

And that...

That was enough to carry me through the rest of the day.

CHAPTER TWENTY-EIGHT

HER GOODBYE WASN'T FINAL

Our days in Dubai had settled into a relentless rhythm. From early morning till evening, we were immersed in closely observing every tiny detail of the client's operations. We documented the workflow meticulously—how their staff managed inventory, how accounts were logged, how payments flowed. For a company of this scale, things could easily slip through the cracks, and we couldn't afford that. We were cautious. Thorough. Almost obsessively so.

But as the sun would set behind the glass towers of Dubai, a different rhythm would take over my mind. One that had nothing to do with code, or clients, or project timelines.

Every night, I'd wait.

For her.

Soumya usually came online after 2:00 AM IST. It had become our unspoken routine—our little sanctuary amid the chaos of work and distance. We'd chat for an hour or two, laugh, tease, share. And if for some reason she didn't show up, I'd find myself restless, scrolling through old chats, rereading every message like it held oxygen.

It had been six days since I landed in Dubai. Work was going smoothly. Even Soumya was being unusually consistent with her updates from her trip. But that night... something felt off.

It was already 2:15 AM here. She hadn't messaged. I figured she was still with Ansh, probably busy laughing, exploring, living her own story. The silence gnawed at me.

Unable to sleep, I opened our old conversations. Scrolling through her quirky lines and emoticons, my heart felt an odd ache—a blend of longing and joy. I missed her. Not just her messages. I missed her. The way she called me *"paglu."* The way she fought with me over the smallest things. The way she made everything feel like it mattered.

By 3:30 AM, I couldn't take it anymore. I knew she was probably asleep. Still, I typed a message. Maybe it was part impulse, part test. Or maybe just a need to feel close.

Me: Hi, I want to tell you something... nothing confirmed yet, just a thought. We are planning to leave India and shift to Dubai permanently. It's a dynamic city—a business hub. What do you think? Suggest! Bye, good night!

I wanted to know if it mattered to her... if I still mattered.

After sending it, I switched off my phone and tried to sleep. Tried.

Morning came with the abrupt ringing of Hitesh's phone. I groggily powered mine on. It was 8:46 AM.

Notifications.

Facebook.

Soumya.

I opened the app with a strange blend of excitement and nervousness.

Soumya: Please, yaar!

Soumya: What am I supposed to do if you're planning to shift??

Soumya: Better don't talk to me!

Soumya: Never!

Soumya: Do whatever you want... I'll prefer to stay out of it.

Soumya: Goodbye...

Soumya: And I'll try my best to make this goodbye the last one!

Her anger crackled through the screen. And yet, instead of hurting, it made me... happy. She cared! Her anger wasn't just anger—it was concern, fear, attachment. Proof that my absence would hurt her.

I immediately replied:

Me: Hey... listen... we haven't decided anything yet. It was just a thought.

Me: We were just talking...

Me: Are you there?

She came online almost instantly.

Soumya: Why the hell are you sharing this with me?

Soumya: Who am I to suggest anything to you??

Soumya: Just do whatever you want!!!

Soumya: Bye!!!

I felt a pinch in my heart. Still, like an idiot, I typed:

Me: Okay... bye... happy now?

I had no idea why I said that. Maybe I wanted her to stop me.

And then...

She was typing again.

Soumya: Yaar maine baat hi kyun ki aapse? (Why did I even talk to you in the first place)

Soumya: I just hate you.

Soumya: Dimag already kharab tha... and now this ruined my mood even more. (My head was already messed up... and now you've completely ruined my mood.)

Soumya: I don't want you in my life anymore.

Soumya: Ever.

My heart dropped. I stared at her words, not knowing what to say.

Me: But why? Okay... I'm not shifting. I'm sorry.

Soumya: What do you even think of yourself?

Soumya: I don't want your drama.

Soumya: You think it's funny? Just like that... you'll shift?!

Me: Wait, Pagal... take a breath...

Soumya: Shut up!

Soumya: Wait for what???

Soumya: Just remember... I'm still angry with you!!

Me: Okay, okay... but we can still talk, right? :D

Soumya: Ab dekh mai kya karti hoon! (Now see what I'm going to do!)

Soumya: If I had more balance, I'd have abused you so much your ears would've rung!!

Soumya: Bye.

Soumya: Halkat aadmi!! (You despicable human!!)

Later that night around 9:30 PM, while having dinner with Hitesh and Dhiraj, my phone buzzed. That familiar Facebook tone. It had to be her.

I replied:

Please wait 30 minutes... eating dinner.

When I logged into Facebook after dinner, her earlier messages were already waiting:

Soumya: Oye... come back by tomorrow! I'm not asking—it's an order! And if you won't follow the order, then it's a request. But I want you back in Bhubaneswar by tomorrow.

Soumya: Got it? I'm on the train right now. Heading back to BBSR.

I smiled. Even in anger, she wanted me close.

Me: Hello, I'm sorry. But tell me, how can I possibly reach there by tomorrow?

She was online again.

Soumya: I don't know! That's your problem!!

Me: Then I need a chartered plane ?

Soumya: Sell your house.

Soumya: I don't care.

Soumya: But be in BBSR by tomorrow. Got it???

Me: Still... to sell my house I need to be home first, na?

Soumya: Shut up!!! You think this is a joke?!

Me: Honestly... even I want to be in Bhubaneswar tomorrow. Just to see you.

Me: Okay, but listen...

Me: Okay, bye.

She went offline.

And I... I sat there, wishing I could hear just a little more from her. Even those silly, sweet curses—her unique way of caring—had become something I secretly longed for. I considered recharging her number, just to provoke another outburst. Just to feel that familiar chaos again.

But I knew better. That would only spark another argument. So I let it go.

And yet, in the middle of all this madness, I felt lighter. Happier. Like I'd been recharged instead. That ridiculous banter—it was her spell, her madness. *Her pagalpanthy.*

Later that night, as the world around me quieted, her message arrived:

Soumya: Kab aa raha hai tu wapas?? (When are you coming back, huh?!)

I read it the next morning, as I opened Facebook.

And I smiled.

Despite being younger, she often spoke to me like we were the same age. Like the eight-year difference between us didn't matter in the least. She always insisted—love and friendship don't come with age restrictions.

And honestly? That side of her—so fiercely innocent, so defiantly affectionate—was utterly, irresistibly adorable.

CHAPTER TWENTY-NINE

HOMELY PUNISHMENT

The morning had already been a whirlwind—stacked with meetings, nonstop calls, and the usual deadlines. Just as I was about to head for lunch, my phone rang. It was my mother.

Mom: "Hi beta, how's everything going? I've got some good news for you!"

Me (after taking her blessings): "All good, Ma. What's the news?"

Mom: "We've been looking for a girl for you, and your papa has finalized the match. She's from a well-respected family. We'll send her photo shortly."

Me: "Okay…"

Mom: "The engagement is on the 3rd of October. You'll be back in India by then, right?"

Me: "Yes, I'll be there."

And that was it. No conversation. No curiosity about what I felt or thought. Just a neatly wrapped decision, handed over like a done deal. I wasn't even surprised—this was classic Papa. A good man, but often impressionable, prone to acting under pressure or someone's persuasion.

Still, I didn't protest. Maybe it was trust in my family. Maybe it was fatigue. Or maybe it was because I didn't have a legitimate reason to say no—at least not one I could put into words. There was no formal commitment with Soumya. No labels, no promises. Just an emotional mess that neither of us ever tried to define. And deep down, maybe I wasn't ready to make such a stand—to say "no," to claim that space for myself, to admit that every unknown face still had to pass a silent comparison test against one girl I could never truly call mine.

While I was halfway through lunch, a WhatsApp message popped up from my younger brother. It was a photo of the girl. Clearly taken from a framed print, the image was grainy. She had a small mole near her right nostril and looked slightly overweight in the picture. Below average—if I had to describe her plainly.

But I wasn't the type to judge someone by a single photo, or by looks at all.

A few minutes later, my brother called.

Brother: "So... how's the photo?"

Me: "It's fine."

Brother: "Did you like the girl?"

Me: "I liked the photo frame."

Brother: laughs "Lol."

Click. He hung up.

I didn't know if he took that as a yes or not, but the abrupt end left me a little unsettled. Hitesh, who was sitting nearby, noticed the shift in my expression.

"What happened?" he asked.

I showed him the photo and explained the situation.

He smiled and said, "Congratulations."

But I didn't respond.

I just finished lunch in silence... and returned to work with a strange emptiness swelling inside.

No phone call came after that. No discussion, no details—nothing.

Not even a word about who she was, what she did, or what her dreams might be. Just a photo. A date. A decision.

What kind of parent finalizes something as life-altering as marriage without even consulting their child?

I had never asked my family for much—if anything at all. I had always played the role of the "good son," the dependable one who chose family's needs over personal choices. The one who never rebelled, never questioned too loudly. Maybe that's where I went wrong.

Maybe I trusted them too much.

Or maybe I was overthinking it all. Perhaps the girl really was a good fit, and I was just being unfairly judgmental based on a single photo taken from a dusty photo frame.

But still... it stung.

Not because of who she was. But because of how little I mattered in the decision.

At that moment, it wasn't about love or compatibility. It was about being handed a life—wrapped in tradition and silence—without a say in what I truly wanted. Without anyone even asking.

And deep down, I knew that wasn't just about marriage.

It was a mirror to every unspoken corner of my life.

—--

With Soumya, things had always been a roller coaster—sharp turns, sudden drops, rare highs. But now, it felt like we were spiraling into a final descent. A slow, steady downfall.

Maybe it was me. I was busy—too consumed with work, too drained to wait endlessly for a simple hi that might never come. Or maybe it was her. She seemed fully immersed in her new world with Ansh, where I no longer fit.

Our conversations had dwindled from hours to minutes, and then to silence. The warmth faded. The teasing, the little fights, the long calls that once felt like lifelines—they had all quietly vanished.

More than anything, I was starting to feel... irrelevant.

Not hated, not ignored. Just unneeded.

And sometimes, that kind of silence hurts more than words ever could

CHAPTER THIRTY

RETURN

9th August, 2014

We bid farewell to Dubai after what had been a truly successful business trip. As a team—and as a company—we had gained tremendously. Not only did we secure a stable stream of income through the ongoing responsibility of maintaining and enhancing their software, but we also created the financial space to finally start focusing on our dream project: a search engine to help people find materials more efficiently.

Before boarding the flight back to Bhubaneswar, I sent a message to Soumya on WhatsApp: *"Heading back today."*
I didn't expect a reply—not anymore—but still, I kept glancing at my phone, hoping to see those two blue ticks. Hoping for a sign that she still cared, even if just enough to read.

At Bhubaneswar Airport, Dr. Patra was there to receive us. His face lit up with joy the moment he saw us. As we made our way out, we shared a brief rundown of our trip—our achievements, the new opportunities, and our plans moving forward. He was genuinely thrilled, and his appreciation felt like a warm welcome home.

That evening, around 7:00 PM, my phone buzzed. It was Soumya.

She informed me that she had enrolled in a coaching institute in Kota for her IIT preparation and would soon be leaving with her father, Mr. Patra. She mentioned she wasn't in Bhubaneswar anymore but had returned to her hometown.

I felt a strange mix of emotions—relief that she chose to tell me, and a quiet sadness at the coldness in her voice. Her tone was distant, almost formal, like she was talking to a colleague rather than someone who once meant so much to her. Still, I wished her the best with all my heart.

For a moment, I considered telling her about my upcoming engagement, about everything that had been happening in my life. But something held me back. Maybe it was pride, maybe fear, or maybe the quiet realization that she wouldn't care the way I wished she would.

We didn't chat at all that day, though I saw her online several times. It hurt—this silence. Especially because she was once furious at the thought of me leaving for Dubai. Now that I was back, it was like my return meant nothing. Her behavior—always so unpredictable—left me confused, and quietly aching.

The next few days were a blur.

I went to work like a machine—automatic, lifeless. Code. Coffee. Meetings. Laughter I didn't feel. Deadlines I didn't care about. My smile? A mask stitched too tight. Even the blinking cursor on my screen felt more responsive than the people around me.

Exactly ten days later, she called.

But it wasn't the call I had been hoping for.

She was furious—blaming me again for something I hadn't done. Apparently, her account had been hacked, and once more, she believed I was behind it.

Like I had nothing better to do. Like I spent my nights plotting ways to break into her privacy.

I didn't even have the courage to defend myself properly. Her words hurt—every syllable like a slap.

I had been aching just to hear her voice, to know how she was doing in Kota, to ask if she was eating well, studying fine.

But she had called only to accuse.

Still, I held back my frustration. I messaged her later, asking her to calm down and explain what exactly had happened.

When we finally talked it through, it turned out her password was something incredibly simple—easy enough for anyone with basic knowledge to guess. It wasn't even hacking. It was just carelessness.

Yet she truly believed it was me.

I helped her recover the account. She thanked me, yes. But it didn't feel like before.

It didn't carry the warmth I used to know. It felt formal, distant—like I was just a stranger who happened to help.

And in that moment, I realized something painful.

I was no longer the most trusted person in her life.

Once, she had said she trusted only me. That I was her lifeline.

Now, I was just another suspect.

I wanted to ask her about Kota, about her classes, about everything she had been experiencing in these last ten days. I wanted to share things from my side too—funny incidents, good news, stories.

But I didn't have the strength anymore.

I was tired of proving my innocence in a story I never wrote.

Anyway, now at least I had her new phone number.

——-

It was around 11:30 PM., I had just stretched out on my bed, trying to find comfort in the late August humidity. The fan above me spun lazily as I scrolled through my phone one last time, hoping for something—anything—to quiet my restless mind., trying to convince myself that sleep might finally come. Out of habit, I checked my phone one last time.

She was online.

On her new number.

I hesitated, then typed:

Me: "Hey..."

The message was delivered. Instantly, the two ticks turned blue.

She was typing.

My heart skipped, expecting... something. Anything that hinted we still shared the same bond.

But then her message appeared:

Soumya: "I'm discussing something related to studies with friends in our study group. It might take time. I'll talk to you later. Bye, good night. Take care."

A pause. Nothing more.

Me: "Okay. Good night."

That was it.

No smiley. No softness. No trace of the warmth that once made me feel like I mattered.

Just cold, measured words.

It wasn't just a message—it was a message between the lines.

"You don't need to message me. You're not a part of this circle anymore."

I kept staring at our chat. Rereading. Replaying the blue ticks. The "typing..." that I had waited for with hope.

Sleep never came.

I lay there for hours, watching her status flicker between "online" and "last seen."

Watching. Waiting. Breaking—silently.

It's strange how one sentence can echo louder than a scream.

And that night, her silence...

It screamed.

CHAPTER THIRTY-ONE

THE ENGAGEMENT TRAUMA

September 7, 2014 – Sunday Morning

I woke up to a call from home. It was Ma. Her voice, cheerful. Mine, reluctant.

"Beta, buy something nice to wear for your engagement. What color and design do you like?"

I had nothing to say that wouldn't sound bitter. So I replied bluntly, *"Any color. Any design. Whatever size bhai wears, it'll fit me too."*

I hung up.

Not a hint of excitement. Not even a flicker.

Everything was decided. Chosen. Purchased. Planned. Except me.

The engagement date was fixed. The girl—someone I'd barely seen. My voice? Unheard.

Papa had always been someone who could be influenced. And this time, the decision was made without even a question. I wanted to protest, to resist. But I didn't. I couldn't.

Why?

Because I wasn't in a relationship with Soumya. Not officially. No proposal. No promise. Just endless emotions, and memories that belonged to no one.

I kept thinking: maybe I'm overreacting. Maybe that girl is kind. Maybe this is how it works in families like ours.

But deep down, I felt like I was being wrapped in silk—only to be buried alive.

A Gift She'd Never Forget(?)

September – Her Birthday Month

September had always felt festive. Because it was her birthday month. Even when she didn't remember I existed.

This year, I wanted to gift her something unforgettable. A digital memory.

She had sent me so many photos—childhood, school, selfies, festival pics. I collected them all and built a private website, secured with login credentials. A tribute to her journey. It wasn't just a project—it was my way of preserving her.

For ten nights straight, I didn't sleep. I coded, compiled, designed.

By the night before her birthday, the site was ready.

September 17, 2014 – Midnight

At exactly 12:00 AM, I dialed her number. Busy.

12:05 AM – Still busy.

I smiled bitterly. I knew. It was Ansh. Of course it was.

12:35 AM – It rang. Three rings. No answer.

I gave up. I collapsed onto my bed and slept—not from peace, but exhaustion.

The Morning After

7:30 AM. My phone lit up with messages. Her tone: furious.

"What do you think of yourself? I'll die if you don't wish me? Keep your ego. Don't call again. Bye forever."

I stared at the words. What?

I called. She picked up instantly.

I explained. I had called. She didn't believe me.

As always, I was the villain.

I took a deep breath, typed a long message explaining everything—and shared the credentials to her birthday website.

She replied:

"Thanks."

Just that. Nothing more. Not even a login confirmation.

I wasn't sure which hurt more—that she didn't see the gift, or that she didn't care.

October 2, 2014 – Hometown

I reached my hometown for what felt like an arranged surrender—my engagement.

It was Durga Puja, a festival I had always adored as a child. But this time, the colors, the lights, the laughter around me—they all felt muted, like they were part of someone else's life.

My mother greeted me with excited eyes. She showed me the clothes she'd selected for me—the heavily embroidered kurta, the matching shoes, even the ring that I'd be exchanging the next day.

No one asked how I felt.

Not once.

No one noticed the silence of the boy who had always filled the house with jokes and stories.

Not one person paused to ask, **"Are you okay?"**

It was as if I were just a groom-shaped prop in someone else's dream.

I tried to remind myself: This is your family. Maybe they know what's right. Maybe you're overthinking.

But my heart wasn't convinced.

October 3, 2014 – The Engagement

At the scheduled time, I reached the venue with my family. I wore the heavy outfit like armor—meant to hide the ache inside. The ring ceremony was quick, mechanical. Smiles were exchanged. Flashbulbs went off.

That was the first time I saw her—the girl I was about to get engaged to.

She looked older in person than in the photograph. A bit heavier too. But I didn't care about appearances.

What stung was the fact that we weren't even allowed to speak to each other.

Not even a moment alone.

Not even a "Hi, I'm Mrinal."

It was all a ritual. No connection. No conversation. No consent that actually felt like mine.

People clapped. They congratulated me. They shook my hand.

But all I wanted to do was disappear.

After a light meal, I asked a close relative to step outside with me—just to "visit a Puja pandal."

As we walked away from the venue, I removed the ring and handed it to him.

"Keep it with you. It's not safe to roam around wearing gold."

That was my excuse. But the truth was, I couldn't bear to wear it.

Not when every part of me was screaming no.

While roaming, I received a call from Hitesh and Dhiraj.

They congratulated me with warmth and laughter.
But I didn't say much.
    They knew me too well.
They knew this wasn't my dream.
They knew I wasn't happy.
    And still, I hadn't told Soumya.
    I didn't have the courage.

CHAPTER THIRTY-TWO

THE RETURN THAT WASN'T A HOMECOMING

The very next day, I told my family I needed to get back to Bhubaneswar—citing pending work as the reason. But the truth was, I couldn't stay any longer. My own home didn't feel like home anymore.

The house where I had grown up, laughed freely, argued playfully... now felt like a stranger's space. Everyone was celebrating, but I felt like a guest at my own funeral. My soul had gone quiet. **I was breaking inside—silently, helplessly.**

Before I left, I remembered how Hitesh and Dhiraj had asked me to bring them some of that homemade chilli pickle they loved so much. But I couldn't even bring myself to ask anyone at home for it. That simple act of asking—something so ordinary—felt too heavy, too intimate, too out of place in a house that no longer felt mine.

I was suffocating.

And the one person I always used to talk to about everything—the one who could lift me out of even my darkest thoughts—was now distant, silent. Soumya didn't ask how I was. Didn't message. Didn't care. Not anymore.

Just before leaving, I hinted to my mother that I didn't quite like the girl they `had chosen. I didn't even get the chance to open up completely.

She cut me off mid-sentence.

"You too have sisters," she said sharply. *"Think what the world will say if someone breaks an engagement. Respect is everything, beta. These things bring shame—not just to you, but to the whole family."*

That was it.

My feelings didn't matter.

My dreams didn't matter.

I didn't matter.

<u>October 5th, 2014 – Bhubaneswar</u>

She called.

Soumya.

It was evening when my phone buzzed. I hadn't expected it.

She had come to know about my engagement — apparently from her father.

Her voice on the call didn't carry sadness. In fact, she sounded almost cheerful. Too cheerful. It didn't sit right.

"So... I heard the news. Congratulations! Finally, you found someone."

I stayed silent for a moment. Her voice carried that familiar playfulness — but it felt forced. Plastic.

"Can I see a photo?" she asked.

My brother had forwarded a few event pictures on WhatsApp, so I simply passed them along.

There was a pause after she saw them.

Then came her reaction — sharp, fast, polished:

"You really liked this girl? I'm happy for you. Truly. Congratulations."

And she hung up.

No tremble in her voice. No hesitation. It felt like she'd been waiting for this day.

Like she could finally breathe.

But I couldn't.

I kept staring at the call log. Wondering what just happened.

Was she really okay? Or just pretending to be?

A few days later...

She called again. This time, the mask cracked.

"Mrinal... I don't know why, but I don't think you're happy."

Her voice was softer now, stripped of the sarcasm.

"I showed your picture to Dadu and Dadi. They said... the girl doesn't look like a match for you. Not that looks matter... but they were saying something about your eyes. You don't look happy."

I didn't respond.

She continued, more hesitant this time:

"If... if you want... I can ask Dadi to speak with your mother. Maybe she can explain you're not comfortable. That this isn't the right decision."

I was stunned.

She wasn't just being polite anymore.

She cared. She noticed.

And in that moment — even if just for a flicker — I felt seen.

It hit me hard—someone from a city I barely belong to could sense I was unhappy.

And yet, my own family... the people I've lived with all my life... they didn't even ask.

October 23, 2014 – Diwali, the Festival of Lights

It was unexpected.

My phone rang. The caller ID showed an unfamiliar number, but something told me it was from her side—my "to-be" in-laws.

I picked up.

A girl introduced herself as the elder sister of the one I was now engaged to. Her tone was polite, almost formal.

Her Sister: *"She wants to wish you for Diwali. I'll pass the phone."*

I hesitated. Then, *"Okay..."*

Me: *"Hi... kaise ho?"*(Hi, how are you?)

Her (softly): *"Main theek hoon... aap?"*(I am doing good...you?)

Me: *"Main bhi theek hoon..."*(I am doing good too.)

Her: *"Didi ne kaha Diwali hai, toh wish kar do..."*(My sister asked to wish you since it is Diwali)

Me (faint smile): *"Haan... Happy Diwali."*

Her: *"Happy Diwali... aap Bhubaneswar mein hi rehte ho na?"*(Do you live in Bhubaneswar, right?)

Me: *"Haan."*(yes)

Her: *"Kaisa sheher hai Bhubaneswar?"* (How is the city Bhubaneswar?)

There it was. The first real attempt at a conversation.

Simple. Polite. Harmless.

But somehow, it didn't feel like a beginning.

It felt like two strangers trying to stitch together words that wouldn't hold.

I replied, *"Bhubaneswar is a beautiful city. The sea is just about an hour's ride from here."*

There was a brief silence.

Then she asked, *"Samundar kaisa dikhta hai? Kya woh nadi se bada hota hai?"*
(How does the sea look? Is it bigger than a river?)

I blinked. Stunned.

A moment of disbelief passed through me. I didn't know whether to laugh or feel sad.

How could anyone—someone even mildly educated—not know whether the sea is bigger than a river? Was this really the person my parents believed would be a good match for me?

I tried to stay polite and explained gently. *"Yes, the sea is much larger. It's endless... not like a river."*

We kept talking. Or rather, she did. Her words were shy but scattered. Then came the next blow to my already declining enthusiasm.

She told me that she had recently learned how to read time on an analogue watch.

"Bas abhi kuch din pehle samjha mummy ne... ghadi me samay kaise dekhte hain."
(Just a few days back, my mother explained how to read time in a clock .)

I didn't know how to respond. I stayed quiet, hoping she wouldn't notice the silence on my end.

She added quickly, almost as if defending herself, *"Padhai ka toh waqt hi nahi mila... mummy hamesha bimar rehti thi."*
(I never got the chance to study... my mom was always unwell.)

I wasn't sure if that was the truth or just an excuse she had learned to say.

Something inside me shut off.

I wasn't trying to be arrogant. But how was I supposed to build a life with someone who didn't even know the basics I had taken for granted as a child? How would she understand my world, my ambitions, my work, my dreams?

My interest in the conversation disappeared. Just like that.

I replied curtly to the next few lines, keeping it civil but distant. Then I politely said I had some work and ended the call.

As the screen went black, I sat still, staring into nothing.

A single thought echoed in my mind:

Why? Why did my parents choose her?

Why this punishment to me...?

The world outside was celebrating light.

But within me, Diwali had never felt darker.

The Unheard Goodbye

That night, I saved her number—not to stay connected, but to ignore it if it ever lit up my screen again.

I had made up my mind.

I would marry her.

Not because I loved her, not because I wanted to...

But because my parents did.

That would be my sacrifice. My obedience. My silence.

But in return, I would light a fire inside myself.

I swore to myself that I would build an empire in five years. Not for legacy. Not for pride.

For closure.

Half of everything I earned, I would give to my family—who never once paused to ask if I was happy.

The other half, I'd hand over to the woman they chose for me—because she'd carry my name, even if she never touched my heart.

And then... I'd disappear.

No long speeches.

No suicide notes.

Just absence.

My happy ending would be quiet.

Because truthfully—this world didn't need me.

Not my family.

Not Soumya.

Not anyone.

I was crying—not visibly, but loudly, violently, deep within.

Each breath felt heavier.

Each heartbeat felt like betrayal.

How did I end up here?

I had been the boy who once believed he could save someone.

Now, I couldn't even save myself.

I stared at the ceiling that night with eyes wide open, yet seeing nothing.

My soul was screaming, but the room stayed still. Silent.

If love had a funeral, I had just attended mine.

CHAPTER THIRTY-THREE

THE CALL THAT BROKE THE SILENCE

November 19, 2014

Days were passing, but not like wind or water. They dragged, like heavy chains.

Yes, professionally I was doing fine—projects delivered, deals closed, money flowing.

But inside, I was sinking.

Overthinking had become my new addiction.

My mind, once a factory of ideas, had turned into a courtroom—haunted by questions with no answers, trials with no verdicts.

I kept returning to the same questions:

Where did I go wrong?

Did she ever care?

Was I ever enough?

There were nights when I thought about ending it all—not out of drama, but out of exhaustion.

But I had responsibilities.

I wasn't a coward.

I made myself a quiet promise:

"When I've fulfilled my duties, I'll quietly disappear. That will be my peace."

Recently, I had noticed something odd—Soumya had vanished. No online below her name in WhatsApp. No activity on Facebook.

It didn't worry me at first.

Maybe she was finally focused on her studies—her exams were just a few months away.

And let's face it—if I mattered so little to her, why would she reach out anyway?

But then... it happened.

That day—November 19th— my phone rang.

It was an unknown number.

My breath caught in my throat.

Could it be her?

Or worse—was it my would-be fiancée again, trying to talk about the weather or how big the sea was?

I answered.

It was Soumya.

From a new number.

Her voice was low—quiet, not because she was tired, but because she was holding something heavy.

She said, "I broke up with Ansh."

And after a pause, "I broke my SIM too."

I didn't ask why. I didn't have to.

But she asked something that melted me.

"Do you have a few minutes to talk?"

She didn't know I had a lifetime for her.

I said, "Yes."

And she began.

She spoke—raw, honest, unfiltered.

She told me how Ansh had started blaming her for everything—his failures, his stress, even his lack of direction.

She shared how his tone turned sharp, his words turned cruel.

How she began to feel worthless.

And then she said the words I'll never forget:

"He told me I'll never become anything in life."

I could feel her breaking as she said it.

But also... I could feel her healing.

Like she had finally pulled out a thorn that had been buried too long.

She cried.

But it wasn't the broken, desperate crying I had once known.

This was different.

It was grief—yes.

But it was also release.

And in that moment, something stirred inside me.

A hope I hadn't dared to feel in months.

A whisper that said:

"Maybe... just maybe... My Soumya is coming back."

<u>Back to Life</u>

For the first time in what felt like ages, I felt alive again.

Just hearing her voice, knowing she still turned to me when things fell apart—it gave me a sense of purpose I thought I had lost.

I still mattered to her.

Maybe not in the way I used to dream of, but in some quiet corner of her life—I was still there.

And the way she spoke, it was clear: she hadn't called anyone else. It was me she trusted. She wanted to talk to.

The best part?

She wasn't broken. Not this time.

There was a calm in her voice—a steadiness. She told me she had left the hostel and returned to her hometown.

"I'll be joining private tuition here," she said. "Still aiming for IIT."

We talked for over two hours that day. Just us. No interruptions. No one stealing her attention mid-call.

For once, the conversation flowed like it used to—effortless, silly, warm.

And then there was this thing she kept doing... every 15 minutes, she'd pause and ask,

"I hope I'm not disturbing your work?"

How could I explain to her...

That the only thing that ever truly disturbed me was her silence?

That her voice was the one "distraction" I'd always welcome—again and again.

She didn't know it.

But in those two hours, she gave me something no one else had in months—
A reason to smile. A reason to breathe.

<u>More Important Than Me?</u>

November 20, the next evening

It was around 4:00 PM. I had just stepped out of a café near CRPF Square when I spotted a familiar face—one of Soumya's distant cousins. We had met once at a family function, and he recognized me instantly.

"Aren't you Mrinal bhaiya? Soumya talks a lot about you," he smiled, shaking my hand.

My heart stuttered at that line. Talks a lot about me? I wanted to ask what exactly she says, but I played it cool. We spoke casually—about my work, the weather, the city. I was careful not to ask anything about her. It felt too close... too risky.

And just then—my phone buzzed.

Soumya Calling.

I panicked for a moment. I couldn't talk freely—not with someone from her family standing right next to me. I answered the call.

"Hello?"

"Where are you?" she asked, her voice light, expectant.

"Hey... I'll call you in a while, okay? Someone's here with me."

"Who?"

"Uhh... your cousin. The one who lives near CRPF Square"

Silence.

Then the line went dead.

At the time, I didn't think much of it. I assumed she got busy or had poor signal. But ten minutes later, my inbox lit up like a Diwali sky.

Soumya:

Oh wow.

So now I'm not even important enough for one full minute of your attention?

You had to cut my call because of HIM?

Amazing.

Your loyalty is so flexible, Mrinal.

Clearly, your priorities are sorted.

I stared at the messages, stunned. Was she seriously angry about this?

I replied cautiously:

Me: "Soumya, what are you even saying? I couldn't talk because your relative was there. Imagine how awkward it would've been. I didn't want to—"

Soumya:

Oh please!

Don't pretend it was about awkwardness.

You've never cut my call before.

Unless I mattered less than the person in front of you.

Me: "Pagal, it was just for a few minutes... I was going to call you right back."

Soumya:

But you didn't.

You chose to make me feel like an option. And trust me—I felt it.

Every second of that silence told me where I stood.

I felt my head spin. How do you explain logic to someone who's not looking for logic—just reassurance? I wasn't even angry. I was helpless. Defeated.

Me: "I didn't mean to hurt you. I just couldn't speak freely in that moment. That's all."

Soumya:

You shouldn't have to choose between me and anyone.

But when you do—choose me.

Even if it makes you look stupid. Even if it's inconvenient. Just... choose me.

Her words stayed with me, long after the conversation ended.

That night, I lay in bed staring at the ceiling fan.

It wasn't about her cousin. Or me cutting the call.

It was about her wanting to feel like she came first. Like she was irreplaceable. Like even a far-off relative wouldn't make me hesitate to talk to her.

And honestly... in her madness, in her fury—I saw something heartbreaking.

She didn't want to be "loved logically."

She wanted to be fought for foolishly.

And that...

That was her pagalpanthy.

CHAPTER THIRTY-FOUR

BETWEEN RIGHT AND REAL

December 4, 2014 8:45 PM.

It was just another evening—at least, that's what I thought. I was riding back from work, lost in traffic and thoughts, when my phone began vibrating incessantly in my pocket. I ignored it at first, thinking it must be some client follow-up.

By the time I reached my room and checked, there was a missed call and a stream of messages.

Soumya: Hellloooo... call kyun nahi uthaya?? (Why didn't you pick up thecall?)

Me: Gadi chala raha tha.(I was riding bike)

Soumya: Ohhh... koi baat nahi. Humne aapko maaf kiya.(Oh , no issue..I forgive you)

Me: So kind of you!

She was clearly in a playful mood. The kind of mood where she didn't want anything—no validation, no topic—just time. Just a conversation. Just me.

Soumya: Acha suno...(ok listen...)

Me: Kya? (what?)

Soumya: Bhaingan ka bharta bana hai aaj! (Bigan ka bharta has been cooked today)

I smiled. These random updates had become their own kind of poetry. We kept chatting—silly things, meaningless things, but all that mattered. She sent me a few selfies and asked if she looked smart.

Me: Not at all.

She pretended to be furious.

Then came a voice note.

"Baba jee ka thullu," she said in her cartoonish voice.

I burst out laughing. That was her—chaotic joy wrapped in contradictions.

Suddenly, her tone shifted.

Soumya: "You're busy with work, right? If it's inconvenient, I can call later... really, it's okay."

Me: No, I'm not working. I'm doing something far more important—something I love.

Soumya: Oye hoye! Hug?

Me: Absolutely.

She meant a virtual hug. But somehow, I felt it in real.

Soumya: Mujhe aisi masti karne mein bada maza aata hai... and I'm obviously comfortable with you... (I love messing around like this... and with you, it just feels easy.)

Soumya: But still... I'm feeling guilty.

Me: Don't. Please don't.

Soumya: Kuch samajh nahi aata... ek toh as friends we're too close and frank. But now, you have someone else in your life.

(I'm so confused... We're so close and honest as friends. But now there's someone else in your life.)

She meant my fiancée. And suddenly, the air between us thickened.

Soumya: I'm sorry. I'm making things difficult for you. But mera haq hai aap pe... par galat bhi hai... Aap mere ho... par reality mein didi ke ho...

(Soumya: I'm sorry. I'm making things difficult for you. But I have a right over you... yet it's wrong too... You belong to me... but in reality, you belong to didi.)

I didn't know how to reply. I didn't want to break her. But I didn't want to lie either.

Me: Soumy, please don't feel guilty. Not if it's just about a hug.

Soumya: I'm not guilty about the hug... I'm guilty about the thought. The feeling that you're still mine... and that I'm wrong to feel that way.

I told her again not to overthink it. But her replies became quieter. Then she said:

Soumya: Don't reply... let me just write. Mujhe bolne do... you do your work. Read later.

Me: Okay...

And she wrote. And every word burned through me like ink on fire.

"Samajhdari ke chakkar mein bahut dialogues maar liye... ab main real Soumya banke bol rahi hoon. Hum kyun dein aapko kisiko aur? Sach mein, I want ki aap dono bahut khush raho. Sab sahi ho jaaye jaldi se... par mujhe khud pe gussa aata hai. Samajhdari ke chakkar mein I keep restricting myself. Tu toh mera tha na? Fir kya hua?"

("In the name of being mature, I've said a lot of things... but now I'm speaking as the real Soumya. Why should I give you to someone else? Honestly, I want you both to be very happy. I hope everything gets better soon... but I get angry at myself. In the name of maturity, I keep holding myself back. You were mine, right? Then what happened?")

I couldn't type. I just stared.

Then she added:

"Simple si baat hai. I hate sharing you. Not even with Hitesh bhaiya. Real Soumya feels like she can do anything with you—hug you, hit you, joke with you—because you're MINE. But Artificial Soumya knows her limits."

("It's simple. I hate sharing you. Not even with Hitesh Bhaiya. The real Soumya feels like she can do anything with you—hug you, fight with you, tease you—because you're mine. But the 'artificial' Soumya keeps reminding me of boundaries.")

That last line sat on my chest like a stone. "Artificial Soumya." The part of her that knew what was "right." And yet, the real one—the broken, messy, honest one—was here right now, typing with her heart bleeding into every line.

I wanted to hug her through the screen.

But I typed nothing.

I just read, over and over again.

Because I knew... this was love in its most helpless form.

She continued texting, her tone now like someone peeling open their soul with trembling hands.

Soumya:

Real Soumya is screaming inside.

She doesn't want to let go.

She wants to steal time, defy logic, erase the world and just keep you.

But Artificial Soumya... she's sitting quietly. Nodding. Saying 'this isn't right'... saying 'let him go.'

She paused.

Soumya:

You know what hurts the most?

Even when I'm being "Artificial," deep down I wish you'd stop me.
I wish you'd say—'Soumya, screw the world. Be mine.'
But you won't. You never do.
And maybe that's what makes you perfect... and unreachable.

I felt something shatter quietly inside me. I didn't even know what to say anymore. Every reply felt too much... or not enough.

And the worst part?

She wasn't wrong.

She was torn between two versions of herself. One bold and vulnerable—the Soumya who once stood at my doorstep with a broom in hand and laughter in her eyes. And the other, cautious and curated—the Soumya shaped by society, family, expectations, the calendar of arranged futures.

And I... I didn't know which version of her to support.

The Real Soumya made my heart race.
The Artificial Soumya made my heart ache.

But wasn't I split too?

One part of me still waited for her at midnight, still searched for her name in every ringtone, still kept the diary where she wrote "Tu toh mera tha na?" under my pillow.
And the other part... was engaged. Promised. Distant. Trapped.

How do two broken halves ever make a whole?

Maybe we were both trying too hard to pretend we hadn't already chosen each other in a world that wouldn't let us.

I finally typed:

Me:
You don't need to fight between versions, Soumya. Both are you. And both are beautiful.
And I don't need just one of you. I'll take you with all your contradictions, confusion, and chaos.
Just don't go silent on me again. I can handle your guilt. Your anger. Your pagalpanthy. But I can't handle your absence.

She didn't reply for a while.

Then finally:

Soumya:
Idiot. Why do you always say the right things at the wrong time?
I miss you. But I'm scared I'll ruin everything.

Me:

You already ruined me, Soumya. And I never complained once.

Me:

Looks like I've already ruined this life for myself...

But if there's something like a next one—

I just wish you'd come to me there.

Not for a few months... not as a borrowed moment...

But for a lifetime.

There was a long pause.

I stared at the screen, wondering if I'd said too much—or not enough.

Then finally, her reply blinked into view:

Her message hit me like a silent storm.

Soumya:

You fool...

Why does that hurt more than anything you've ever said?

I kept staring at those words, rereading them—again and again.

There was no emoji this time. No dramatics.

Just pain. Raw, unfiltered.

Maybe that's what we were now—two broken pieces trying to be whole for each other... but too late, or too lost, or too tangled in the mess we didn't know how to escape from.

I wanted to say something back—something comforting, something stupid, anything.

But for the first time, I had no words left.

My fingers hovered over the keyboard... then fell away.

All I could do was breathe. And think.

Of all the midnight laughs.

Of all the shared dreams we never got to live.

Of all the unsaid feelings we stitched between jokes and jabs.

Of all the versions of "us" that could have been.

And I thought—

If love was a straight line, maybe we were a spiral. Always returning to each other, yet never at the same point.

I wanted to scream into the silence:

I would have fought the whole world for you... if only you'd asked me to.

But she didn't. And maybe she never would.

Maybe some people aren't meant to be chapters.

They're bookmarks—always holding your place in a story you can't finish, because a part of you still lives on that page.

I closed my eyes.

And whispered quietly to no one...

"If there's a next life...

Don't come late."

Just knowing that my Soumya was still there somewhere beneath all the layers... it was enough.

I knew she wasn't mine — not in this lifetime.

I knew the joy I felt was fleeting, fragile.

But for those few minutes, it felt like I had lived an entire life with her.

And if everything ended right there,

I wouldn't regret a thing.

December 14, 2014 – At Our New Office

The Dubai project—our team's most ambitious assignment yet—was finally delivered after its final round of UAT testing. We had worked tirelessly for weeks, and the results spoke for themselves. The client was beyond satisfied. Not only did we deliver on time, but we exceeded expectations—so much so that they rewarded us with a 10% bonus. The office was buzzing with joy and pride.

As if that wasn't exciting enough, our dream project—an in-house "Search Engine to Find Your Things"—was now ready in its MVP form. It wasn't perfect yet, but it was functional and promising enough to open doors. In fact, early discussions for seed funding had already begun. Everything was slowly falling into place.

Overwhelmed with happiness, I dialed Soumya's number. When she answered, I couldn't wait to share the news.

Me: "Guess what? We've delivered the Dubai project and the client is so happy they gave us a bonus. And our MVP is ready too!"

She: "Congratulations! Now hand over everything you earn... after all, you earn only for me, right?"

Me (laughing): "Then what about my expenses?"

She (without missing a beat): "Fine. I'll give you ₹100. Don't spend it all at once!"

It was classic Soumya—teasing, playful, and effortlessly light-hearted. That short exchange lifted my already high spirits to a new level. It reminded me why I looked forward to talking to her, even on my best days.

9:00PM

I was just a few minutes away from home when my phone rang. It was her—my Soumya.

Her voice came in soft but urgent. *"You're not... drinking, right?"*

I was taken aback. *"What? No, of course not."*

She continued, clearly uneasy. *"I just thought... maybe you'd celebrate today—with Hitesh Bhaiya and Dhiraj Bhaiya... I don't know. Alcohol or something..."*

There was silence for a moment.

Then, she said something that shook me.

"Promise me... promise me you'll never smoke or drink. Not even once. If you care for me—if you've ever loved me, even a little—then don't ever do it. Because if you do... I swear I'll die."

Her words hit me like a storm. They weren't dramatic—they were desperate, pleading, vulnerable. It wasn't about alcohol. It was about me—about what I meant to her, even if she never admitted it in those exact words.

I closed my eyes for a second, letting the weight of her fear settle.

"I promise, Soumya. As long as you're in this world... I'll never break that promise."

And that was it. No oath in front of God, no witness needed.

Just her voice, my silence, and a promise etched forever into my heart.

December 15, 2014

My phone rang—an incoming call from home. It was my mother.

She sounded cheerful, almost festive. *"Beta, we've finalized the wedding date—it's on 18ᵗʰ April next year! You'll need to come home for your suit measurements."*

I didn't say anything for a moment. It felt like she was asking me to give measurements not for a wedding suit... but for a coffin.

Me: "Whatever color my brother picks... and whatever size fits him—it'll fit me too. I'm too busy to come for all this right now."

She paused, then gently insisted: ***"At least come ten days before the wedding. There are so many rituals. You have responsibilities."***

Me: "Okay," I replied—just to avoid another round of emotional blackmail.

But in truth, I had no excitement. No curiosity. No spark.

The wedding felt less like a celebration and more like a sentence—something I had to serve, quietly, obediently.

Later that evening, I told Soumya about the finalised date of my marriage.

She was silent for a moment—too brief to catch, too long to ignore.

Then, with her usual playfulness masking something I couldn't quite name, she said,

"I'd love to attend—if I'm invited."

I didn't know how to respond.

The truth was, I didn't want to invite anyone. Not even my closest friends. Not Hitesh. Not Dhiraj.

Because for me, this wasn't a celebration.

It was a formality.

A ceremony I was sleepwalking into.

A chapter I hadn't chosen to write.

I simply smiled at her message. But inside, I wondered if she truly meant what she said...

Or if that too was her way of saying goodbye.

CHAPTER THIRTY-FIVE

THE SEPARATION

New Year's Eve – A Rose Before the Storm

The New Year was approaching—but unlike the excitement it usually brought, I felt only dread. 2015 loomed like a storm cloud, marking the year of my unwanted marriage. In the midst of that suffocating reality, Soumya remained the only ray of light—flickering, maybe, but still alive in the darkness of my personal life.

Yet, even that light felt fragile. I was terrified she would drift away. That she'd stop caring. That she'd stop replying altogether.

And slowly, my fears began to take shape.

On the 31ˢᵗ of December, I traveled to a nearby city, not far from my hometown. A childhood friend had invited me to his new home for a small New Year gathering, and we had also planned a short four-day trip to revisit places from our childhood.

During the journey, Soumya and I stayed connected over WhatsApp. As midnight approached, she texted saying the New Year was just minutes away and she was rummaging through her messy room, trying to find Pudin Hara for a stomach ache. With a giggle, she joked that her New Year celebration would be all about finding that one strip of medicine.

Amid the banter, she added she had picked up something for me. "It's just 20 rupees," she said, "but I hope you'll like it." She promised to reveal what it was exactly at midnight.

Our conversation was light and playful—like the old days. But as the clock crept closer to twelve, something changed. Something subtle... something special.

At exactly 12:00 AM, just as the world erupted in fireworks and countdowns, Soumya sent me a photo.

She was holding a single red rose in her hand, accompanied by a message:
"Happy New Year! This is the first gift of 2015—from me to you."

It wasn't just a flower. It was a moment frozen in time—a silent, fragrant promise. It felt like she had planned it just for me.

And for a brief moment, I forgot everything else.
The marriage. The distance. The fear.
All I saw... was that rose.

The Kamli Clash

I reached Bokaro that morning, at my friend's place. My own home was just 40 km away—but those 40 km felt like 4000. I had no plans to visit. Not now. Not with this weight in my chest.

The days that followed New Year began warmly. Soumya was talking to me more regularly again—sending voice notes, jokes, little updates. It felt like we were healing.

But sometimes, even the smallest spark can ignite a fire.

One evening, she sent me a YouTube link.

"Watch this. Kamli song dance video. Isn't she amazing?"

I clicked it. A mesmerizing performance—bold, expressive, full of life. She messaged again a few minutes later:

"I wish someone could train me like that. Maybe I could become a dancer... or even an actress in Bollywood someday. I really want to try."

She wasn't joking. I could tell—this was her dream, tucked away in a quiet corner of her heart.

And me? Being the "responsible" one, I replied with what I thought was the sensible thing:

"It's a great idea. But maybe after your exams, okay? Focus on studies for now—this can come later."

It was meant to be caring. Grounded. But I didn't realize the weight my words carried—or the hope they crushed.

A long pause.

Then, her reply:

"You too?"

"I only share these dreams with you... and you also want me to become just another IIT ranker?"

"You don't even care about what I want."

Before I could respond, soften the blow, or explain, the next message came:

"Don't call me again."

Then—blocked.

The online below her name vanished. Her last seen disappeared. And just like that, she was gone.

I was stunned. My fingers trembled as I dialed her number.

It rang.

No answer.

I texted:

"I didn't mean it like that. Please talk to me."

"You know I care. I always have. Please don't do this."

No reply.

I kept checking. Hoping she'd unblock me. Hoping she'd just talk.

But the silence was loud. Brutal. Final.

And it hit me—dreams aren't always about careers or ambition.

Sometimes, they're about being heard.

Supported.

Believed in.

And in that one careless moment...

I had failed her.

CHAPTER THIRTY-SIX

THE UNHEARD APOLOGY

The next morning, I woke up and instinctively checked my phone—half-hoping I had dreamed it all. But no, she was still gone. Blocked. No profile picture. No status. No last seen. Nothing.

I opened our old chats. Scrolled. Re-read the last conversation a dozen times. I kept telling myself it was just a small disagreement—an impulsive reaction. But the silence that followed was unbearable. It wasn't like her. Or maybe, it was like her... when she was deeply hurt.

Two days passed without a word from her. I didn't call—partly afraid she was still angry, partly distracted by the presence of my friend. But inside, I was spiraling. I kept texting her—short, hopeful messages, like fragile paper boats sent into a storm. A part of me wanted to give her space, but another part feared losing her completely. That quiet war inside me made each hour heavier than the last. Small messages. Silent attempts to reach her.

"Good morning. Just letting you know I'm still here."

"I'm sorry, Soumya. I was wrong to dismiss your dream."

"I miss you. Please talk to me once. Just once."

Still, no reply.

That week, I couldn't focus on work. I couldn't sleep properly either. I was constantly staring at my phone screen—wishing for that familiar word online below her name to appear.

Then came the day I was to return. Bags packed, heart heavy, I was about to catch my train when my phone rang.

It was her.

I froze.

"Hello?" I picked up, my voice almost a whisper.

"I saw your messages," she said, calmly.

Those words, so simple, felt like a drop of rain on scorched earth. I didn't know what to feel first—relief that she still acknowledged me, or regret for how easily I had hurt her. My breath caught, and for the first time in days, I felt something shift inside me. Maybe it was hope. Maybe it was just the comfort of her voice. But it was enough to make me believe—maybe not everything was lost.

I didn't know what to say. My silence filled the space.

She continued, *"I was really hurt. Not because you asked me to focus on studies. But because I expected you to be the one person who'd never laugh at my dreams. Who would at least listen."*

"I didn't laugh," I said quickly. *"I just reacted like a stupid elder. I should've listened first. Supported you. Even if it was unrealistic. I'm sorry."*

"I know," she replied. *"But sometimes, knowing isn't enough. We just want someone to believe in us blindly. Without logic. Just love."*

"I'll be that person for you. Always."

She was silent for a moment.

Then finally:

"Don't say 'try.' Just be."

That one line didn't just end the conversation—it etched itself into my mind like a turning point. For days I had been surviving on regret, but now something cracked open. Maybe it was clarity. Maybe it was a second chance. Whatever it was, it whispered that from this moment on, I needed to stop carrying the weight of what went wrong, and start being the man who simply is—for her, and for myself.

And with that—she unblocked me.

No more blame. No long explanations.

Just that one word: "Be."

I smiled. *"Thank you for coming back, Soumya."*

Her reply came with a soft laugh. *"I'm a shameless person. I'll keep coming.".*

It was playful, familiar—like nothing had changed, even though everything had.

"I'm about to catch my train now," I told her, glancing at the platform clock. *"Will WhatsApp you once I settle in."*

"Okay," she said, and we hung up.

I boarded the train just as the sun began leaning west—half hidden, like it wasn't ready to end the day either.

My seat was by the window. I placed my bag under it and settled in. Noise blurred around me—vendors shouting, steel clanking, a baby crying somewhere—but inside, it was quiet.

I opened WhatsApp. "Window seat, like always. Train just left the platform."

Two blue ticks.

Then, her reply:

"Click a photo of the sky for me."

I did.

And in that one photo—just sky and wires and nothing special—I realized how even the ordinary becomes sacred when someone else waits for it.

A few days later, she sent me a message. Just a phone number. No context.

"Do you know this number?"

I checked. *"Nope. Why?"*

"I just got a missed call from it. Thought maybe it's you... from another number."

I smiled. *"No, if I had another number, I'd have called to say something stupid."*

She laughed. Short. Faint.

That was it.

But something about it stayed with me. Like when you smell smoke but can't find the fire.

A few days passed. Then she brought it up again.

"That number... it belongs to a boy. He's been calling often."

"Should I call him? Warn him not to disturb you?"

"No," she replied quickly. *"I'll handle it."*

That "I'll" was new. Sharper. Firmer. Slightly distant.

After that, something began to shift.

Nothing loud. No fights. No drama.

Just... space.

Replies took longer. Smiley counts dropped. "Paglu" didn't come up anymore.

When I asked if everything was okay, she said yes.

But even her yes had started sounding like no.

And then one day, she said it.

"That number? It was Avi's. He's the younger brother of one of my friends."

"We've become good friends now."

Simple. Plain. Like she was just stating a fact.

And somehow, even after the door had closed, I still found myself knocking.

I threw myself into work—more than I usually did. There were two reasons for it: one, whenever I had free time, my thoughts kept circling back to Soumya. I found myself checking her WhatsApp status constantly—not because she was reaching out, but simply because I missed her. And two, I didn't want to think about the bleak, uncertain future that awaited me after marriage.

Soumya still used to call me—once a day, maybe for ten minutes—but it felt more like a formality than genuine need or affection. I knew I had no real right over her. She wasn't doing anything wrong. Even choosing to drift away for someone else wasn't unfair—after all, I was already engaged. Maybe, in her eyes, our story had no future anymore.

But still, something inside me was quietly breaking.

I had started overthinking everything—texting her rudely over things she probably didn't even do intentionally. It became my new normal.

I wasn't working. Just pretending to be busy—using it as a distraction, not a direction..I felt like I was slowly losing my grip—losing my mind.

Maybe I was unable to fully accept that Soumya had her own life, her own choices—and the right to move on. I was no one to her anymore. No commitment. No promises. She was never really mine. But the pain of losing her still felt like I was losing my life—long before I ever intended to end it myself.

Nothing seemed to be working for me anymore.

<u>18th January, 2015 – The Doomsday</u>

I saw them online.

Both of them—Soumya and Avi.

And then I saw my message to her from the previous day. Seen. But unanswered.

That silence hit harder than any spoken word ever could.

A lump formed in my throat. I tried to stay calm, tried to act mature, but something inside me cracked. The ache of being ignored, the fear of becoming irrelevant—it was too much.

I lost control.

Fueled by impulse and emotion, I typed a long message. Sarcastic. Bitter. And yes—immature. I accused her of lying. Of changing. Of pushing me out for someone she barely knew—a boy from a missed call.

"I knew this day would come," I wrote. *"That you'd stop replying, stop caring, that I'd become just another 'past chapter' for you. I just didn't think it would come this soon. And for someone you barely knew... someone who just happened to call."*

I don't even remember all the words I typed. I just remember how my fingers trembled. How my chest felt like it was collapsing with every sentence. I was crying—and yet I couldn't stop.

Her reply came quickly.

But it wasn't the reply I needed.

"What do you even think of yourself? You only know how to accuse and blame. Is your mentality really this cheap—toward a friend of mine? I shared every part of myself with you. You were my support, my closest person. And now, just because I've been a little distant, you're showing your true colors?"

"Yes—Avi is my boyfriend. And yes, I'll spend my life with him. Did you ever have the courage to accept me or even think about marrying me? No, right?"

"So do whatever you want. Consider this my last message. I'll never contact you again. Ever."

"Be happy."

And that was it.

A second later, the screen blinked.

Blocked.

Just like that, she was gone.

Again.

But this time... it felt final.

CHAPTER THIRTY-SEVEN

THE SOUND OF BLOCKED SILENCE

For a while, I just sat there.

Phone still in hand.

Screen still on.

No more typing bubbles.

No more online below her name.

No more Soumya.

I blinked. Once. Twice. But nothing changed.

She was gone.

I stared at our last conversation, reading her words again and again until they blurred into static.

My vision fogged. My fingers numbed. My heart—heavy, loud, and painfully slow.

This wasn't how it was supposed to end.

Not after everything we had been through.

Not after every "babu," every joke, every long night spent making each other feel alive.

Not after that hug.

Not after that rose on New Year's.

I had said hurtful things.

She had said unforgivable ones.

But the silence that followed... that was the most violent.

I sat on the floor.

Phone beside me.

Unmoving.

I didn't cry like a hero in a tragic movie.
I just... collapsed.
Internally.
I felt hollow. Like something had been scooped out from inside and replaced with nothingness.
The world around me faded into a slow, colorless blur.
Notifications came and went.
Client emails. Missed calls. A message from my mother.
But none from her.
Never again from her.
She had shut the door. Locked it. Burnt the key.
And I had no strength left to knock again.

The silence in my room grew louder.
I closed my eyes, hoping for darkness, but instead, my mind lit up with a memory.
Her voice.
That infectious, mischievous laugh.
Her fingers brushing the corner of my desk as she said, "Your room's always so messy!"
That evening. That hug.
The way she leaned in, crying softly against my shoulder...
The way I wiped her tears with my thumb and kissed her forehead—not out of impulse, but as if it had always been the most natural thing to do.
She didn't move.
Didn't speak.
Just smiled with her eyes closed.
Like the world had disappeared and we were suspended in that moment forever.
"You're mine, na?" she had asked.
"Even if everything else changes?"
I had nodded.
I thought I had meant it.
But now? Everything had changed. And she was no longer mine.

26th January – A Glimpse, Then Gone Again
I had stopped checking her WhatsApp by now.

There was no point. She was gone—just like she said she would be. Her number had been silent for days. My birthday had passed too—no message, no missed call, not even a blank "Hi."

It was the first time in years that her absence felt louder than any presence.

But then, on the morning of 26th January, my phone buzzed with a WhatsApp status notification.

Soumya had unblocked me.

My heart skipped.

I tapped, unsure if I was ready for whatever I'd see.

It was a Republic Day post—a quote in bold, colorful font:

"For a man, his lady is his powerhouse. If we empower girls, imagine how powerful a man can become!"

I stared at it for a long while. I opened my diary—yes, the one I used to fill with her statuses, screenshots, memories.

And I wrote beneath it:

"Huh. All bullshit.

I was empowering you, na?

And you became so powerful that you just... threw me out of your life."

There were no messages from her. Not even a hint of apology or check-in. I realized then—she hadn't unblocked me to talk. Probably, just to see if I had messaged her after her dramatic exit.

But there were none.

I hadn't messaged her.

I couldn't.

Within hours, she had blocked me again.

Gone. Like a ghost checking her own grave.

And I was left again in that limbo—where I could neither move on, nor hold on.

9th April, 2015

It had been nearly 75 days since I last spoke with Soumya. Seventy-five days of silence. Of absence. Yet not a second had passed when I didn't think of her. Miss her. Ache for her. Still, somehow, I never found the courage to even send a message.

And today—of all days—I was on a train back to my hometown... for my marriage.

A marriage that had become nothing more than a formality.

As the train slowly pulled out of Bhubaneswar Station, I felt my chest tighten. My vision blurred. My eyes gave in—tears fell without warning. Her memories came flooding in like a monsoon. I saw her smile, her sarcasm, her voice in voice notes. And then, like a cruel contrast, came the haunting image of my future—one I had never asked for.

Everything felt like I was being dragged into a dark, endless tunnel—against my will. With every mile the train covered, I felt more disconnected from myself.

A terrifying thought surfaced—What if the train just... crashed?

What if, somehow, it ended everything right here?

Not to hurt anyone else. Just me. Just a quiet exit. A silent escape. It would spare two lives from misery. Or maybe just one now—the girl I was supposed to marry.

I felt like I had already died inside. The only person who had ever given me life, who made me feel alive again... was Soumya. But she was gone. And I was about to enter a life where even pretending to smile would be a daily struggle.

I closed my eyes and made a wish.

A selfish, desperate, broken wish.

But the next morning, my train reached its destination. Safe. On time.

No accident. No miracle.

Just silence.

God, it seemed, wasn't listening anymore.

CHAPTER THIRTY-EIGHT

THE CALL I NEVER EXPECTED

That night, back in my hometown, I went up to the terrace after dinner. It was around 10 PM, the air unusually still, my mind drowning in everything I was being forced to accept.

And then, my phone rang.

The name flashing on the screen sent a jolt through my entire body—Soumya.

For a split second, my heart raced with a foolish, desperate hope. Maybe... just maybe, she's calling to stop this wedding. Maybe she wants to say she loves me, that she wants to spend her life with me.

And in that single second, I had decided: If she asked, I would leave everything. Right now. For her.

I picked up.

Her voice was soft, hesitant.

"Sorry for calling..." she said.

That broke something inside me.

The one person I longed to hear from... was apologizing just for calling.

She sounded disturbed. *"I... I saw something. Something very strange and... scary."*

I stayed silent, listening.

"I was using Papa's phone," she said, *"and when I opened Chrome, some really dirty websites popped up. I didn't even know things like that existed. It was disgusting."*

She was sobbing quietly.

And in that moment, nothing else mattered. Not my marriage. Not the distance. Just her pain.

I tried to calm her. *"It's possible he accidentally clicked on something malicious—those sites often open automatically from ads. Please don't jump to conclusions. It doesn't necessarily mean what you think it means."*

She was quiet for a moment. Then, softly: *"Maybe you're right..."*

Her breathing slowed. I could sense her calming down.

"I'm sorry again for calling," she whispered.

"No," I said. *"Thank you for calling. Really."*

Then she laughed lightly, wiping away her own awkwardness.

"Main bahut besharam hoon," she said playfully.

"Itni aasani se aapka peecha nahi chhodne wali."

("I'm too shameless. I'm not going to let go of you that easily.")

And just like that, my heart smiled again—for the first time in days.

She asked me where I was.

"At home," I said. *"For the wedding."*

There was silence for a second, maybe two.

Then she said she'd have dinner and hung up the call.

I knew she would call **Avi** next.

But that didn't matter.

Because when something truly scared her, when she needed comfort, it was still me she turned to.

And that, in a way I couldn't explain, still meant everything.

CHAPTER THIRTY-NINE

THE FINAL NOTE

A few days later, I noticed something unexpected—she had unblocked me on WhatsApp.

My heart jumped. But even then, I didn't have the courage to send a simple "Hi."

I stared at her chat window for minutes. Typed. Deleted. Typed again.

Then suddenly, a message popped up from her side. Followed by an audio file.

"This song is dedicated to you," she wrote.

I didn't waste a second. I plugged in my earphones and hit play.

It was her voice.

"Lag ja gale... ke phir yeh haseen raat ho na ho..."

("Come, embrace me... for this lovely night might be our last.")

Her soft, magical voice wrapped around the haunting lyrics of the classic Lata Mangeshkar song.

A melody of parting.

A love too fragile to last.

A plea to hold each other—one last time—before the moment slipped away forever.

I listened, frozen.

And when the final note faded, I replied instantly:

"Your voice... it's beautiful. Truly. Thank you."

But she didn't reply.

Not that night. Not the next day.

And then I realized...

That song wasn't just a dedication.

It was her way of saying goodbye.

A goodbye wrapped in a lullaby.
A farewell she couldn't say in words—so she sang it instead.
And just like that... she was gone again.

<u>April 18 – The Call</u>
It was April 18.
My house was full of guests — laughing, teasing, exchanging jokes. Today was the day. The day. And yet, to me, it felt like the saddest day of my life.

They were preparing me for the baraat, but I felt nothing. No excitement. No joy. Just a growing silence inside me.

Then I heard it — a WhatsApp notification. I checked my phone absentmindedly.

It was Soumya.
Of course it was.

She always knew when to show up — like a ghost of choices not taken. Some days she vanished like she had buried me. Other days, like today, she returned... just when I was about to belong to someone else.

The message was short:
"Can you call me once?"
For the first time, I needed an excuse to talk to her. I wasn't even sure why she wanted me to call. Was her Facebook hacked? Did she need help with something else? I told a relative — who was busy telling me something pointless about wedding rituals — that I had an urgent office call.

I rushed to the terrace and found a quiet corner.
I called her.
She picked up almost instantly.

There was a pause... and then she spoke, softly:
"Can you... just stay on the call during the entire ceremony? Even if you can't talk. I just... I just want to be connected. Don't disconnect. Keep your phone battery full."

She didn't cry. She didn't explain.

She just wanted to be there — as a voice, a presence, a silent echo — while I was being taken away.

I never truly understood Soumya. I don't think I ever will.
But I said yes.

"Okay. I'll keep the call connected."

I didn't know what she wanted to hear, but I kept her on the line — talking to her whenever I could during the baraat. I wasn't really present. I didn't notice who was dancing in front of my car. I didn't care how many firecrackers burst or how loud the music played.

All I heard was her — her voice, soft and distant.
I kept describing the rituals to her like a tour guide walking through his own goodbye.

At some point, the battery must have died. I didn't notice.
I was pulled into the chaos of ceremonies — garlands, blessings, and eventually, the seven rounds around the sacred fire.

I followed every instruction like a machine.
Smile here. Fold hands there. Walk now. Sit now.

But inside?

Nothing.

No excitement.
No butterflies.
No sense of arrival.

Just a strange emptiness dressed in silk and gold.

And now... I was married.

CHAPTER FORTY

THE NIGHT AFTER THE NOISE

The rituals were over.

The noise had died. The guests had left or fallen asleep in spare rooms. The lights in the mandap were still flickering, but my heart... had long powered down.

The room was filled with garlands and awkward silence. My wife sat beside me — quiet, uncertain, rehearsing the role of a new bride. I wanted to say something kind, something gentle.

But I couldn't.

Not tonight.

After a few formal sentences — about being tired, about needing to wake early for more rituals — I stepped away with my phone.

I sat on the edge of the bed, turned the screen on.

Dead.

Not the battery — I had charged it. But there were no new notifications. No missed call.

No message.

No "Did you reach?"

No "Are you okay?"

Nothing from her.

Maybe the call had ended when the phone died earlier.

Maybe she had waited for a while.

Maybe she had cried.

Maybe she had smiled.

I would never know.

I plugged in the charger, unlocked the phone.

Checked WhatsApp.

Last seen — Soumya: 1:26 AM.

Hours before the wedding even began.

Had she ended the call first?

Was she really listening at all?

Had she already made peace... while I was still burning inside?

I sat there, surrounded by jasmine and rituals, feeling more alone than I ever had.

I was married.

And yet, the only person I wanted to talk to... wasn't there.

The Second Day

Soumya wouldn't call again for quite some time.

And perhaps that was for the best.

Because what followed... was something even silence couldn't soften.

It was the second day of my marriage.

My wife — sitting quietly, trying to decode me — finally spoke.

Her voice was gentle, unsure, but carried something... strange.

"Papa told me... if nothing works out, I should just file for divorce."

I looked at her, stunned.

Divorce? Already?

Two days. We hadn't even finished unpacking. We hadn't even had a real conversation.

And she was already talking about endings.

I didn't respond right away.

Maybe I didn't know how.

Or maybe, deep down, I knew she was just saying aloud what I was already thinking in silence.

But still — who prepares their daughter like that?

What kind of father arms a bride with an exit strategy on the second day of marriage?

Instead of bridging the gap between us, her words built a wall.

My interest in her — already shallow, already forced — sank even lower.

Not because of who she was.

But because of who I wasn't.

I wasn't ready. I wasn't willing.

And worst of all, I wasn't there — not emotionally, not mentally.

Every second I spent in that house — my house — felt like punishment.

Like I was wearing someone else's life.

Smiling for people I didn't want to smile for.

Pretending to care about things that meant nothing to me.

I told my family I needed to return to Bhubaneswar — that work needed me.

But the truth was simpler.

I needed to breathe.

And I couldn't do it here.

\-

The train rattled on, carrying me back to Bhubaneswar.

I sat by the window, watching the blur of towns and fields pass by. The same cities we once passed through — during late-night chats and early-morning calls — now moved like strangers.

Somewhere between stations, I remembered:

Soumya's IIT Prelims exam was on April 11th.

It struck me suddenly. Not because I had marked the date. But because some part of me still counted time in relation to her.

And now... it was nearing the 27th. The result would be out soon.

But she hadn't mentioned the exam.

Not before.

Not after.

No "Wish me luck."

No "It was hard."

No "It's over."

Nothing.

Maybe it didn't matter to her anymore.

Or maybe... I didn't.

I opened Facebook to distract myself.

Just mindless scrolling. But then a post caught my eye:

"If a man realizes that a woman cannot live without him, he will devote his entire world to her.

But if a woman realizes that a man cannot live without her...

she can make his life miserable."

It hit me like a punch.

Was that true?

Or was I just the wrong kind of man... loving the wrong kind of way?

CHAPTER FORTY-ONE

RETURN AND DEPARTURE

I reached Bhubaneswar in the morning.

Hitesh was there at the station to receive me. He smiled, asked the usual questions — how was the marriage, did I like her, how was the food, the rituals...

But he didn't ask about celebrating anything.

He already knew.

He could see it in my face — I was tired. Not just physically, but tired of pretending.

Over breakfast, I told him everything.

My decision to leave Bhubaneswar.

My plan to shift to Hyderabad — not for expansion, not for growth — just for escape.

I expected him to argue.

He didn't.

In fact, he nodded.

"Tech Mahindra offered me a transfer to Hyderabad too," he said. ***"I didn't take it earlier because of the startup. But if you're shifting... maybe it's time."***

He didn't ask if I was okay.

He knew I wasn't.

And then he said something else — almost casually:

"Our startup's still not making much profit anyway. Maybe a new city will bring new energy."

I knew that wasn't about profits.

That was about me.

He was being kind.

The truth was, I hadn't been able to focus. I had been distracted. I was holding the whole team back.

Maybe shifting cities wouldn't fix everything.

But it might help... something.

A new place. New rhythm. New silence.

Part of me suspected this plan was already cooked between Hitesh and Dhiraj.

They probably saw this coming — saw me crumbling from the inside, even before I admitted it to myself.

And I was grateful.

They weren't just saving the business.

They were saving me.

CHAPTER FORTY-TWO

THE ESCAPE TO HYDERABAD

I decided to leave the city.

Bhubaneswar — the place that once gave me dreams, a startup, and her — had turned into a graveyard of memories.

Every corner whispered her name.

Every streetlamp flickered with the echo of her voice on the other end of late-night calls.

I couldn't breathe there anymore.

So I moved to Hyderabad.

Not for work.

Not for ambition.

Just to go farther... from Soumya.

It wasn't distance I needed — it was silence.

Detachment.

Anything to stop me from checking her last seen, walking past the spots we once stood in, or wondering if she still remembered my birthday.

Deep down, I had accepted it —

Soumya had chosen her world.

And maybe Avi was part of it now.

I had no right to haunt her story anymore.

And as for mine?

My marriage was already standing on a cracked floor.

My wife had hinted at divorce — as casually as one returns a product that doesn't fit.

Maybe she was right.

Maybe I didn't fit anywhere.

And a part of me thought — if this ends too, maybe that would make things easier.

One less responsibility.

One less person to disappoint.

One less guilt to carry.

If she walks away, I won't stop her.

And maybe then... quitting everything — quietly, permanently — would feel a little less selfish.

Because when nothing holds you back anymore,

letting go doesn't feel cruel.

It feels... peaceful.

One Last Visit

Before leaving Bhubaneswar for good, I made one last stop.

That evening, I went to meet Dr. Patra.

I carried a box of sweets with me — part tradition, part formality. It didn't mean anything to me, but it was expected.

"I just got married," I said with a half-smile, offering the box.

He congratulated me warmly — unaware of the weight behind my words.

I didn't linger on the topic.

I moved straight to the point.

"We're planning to shift to Hyderabad. Better opportunities. Wider exposure."

He nodded thoughtfully.

"That's a good move. You'll find better talent there. Maybe even better funding. Let me know if you need anything."

He didn't ask why I was really leaving.

Didn't ask if I was happy.

Or maybe... he chose not to.

Either way, he wished me well.

And I thanked him — sincerely.

As I stood up to leave, I glanced toward the hallway — almost involuntarily.

Searching for a face I didn't want to admit I missed.

But Soumya wasn't there.

Not in the kitchen.

Not on the stairs.

Not behind the curtain like old times.

The house — once full of her presence — now felt formal, hollow.
A moment later, Dr. Patra said casually:
"Soumya's gone to her ancestral home for a few days."
He didn't say where.
I didn't ask when she left.
We let silence fill in the blanks.
And just like that...
the last chapter in that house closed itself.

CHAPTER FORTY-THREE

BETWEEN TWO CITIES

We had three months of rent left on our Bhubaneswar office.

So we decided to keep it running — for now.

Let the team continue operations. Let the place stay alive while Hitesh and I began our gradual shift to Hyderabad.

Whether we'd keep that office beyond three months — we weren't sure.

Maybe we'd shut it down.

Maybe we'd go fully remote.

It all depended on what Hyderabad offered — in talent, in cost, in opportunity.

Truth was, we had to cut down costs to survive.

Our in-house product — the one we believed in more than anything — was bleeding us dry without generating returns. We were almost out of stretch.

So I started sending out emails again — the bold kind.

One to Apple Computers, pitching the core idea of our product.

Not expecting a reply. Just... needing to try.

Several to venture capitalists — chasing the same fragile hope every founder lives on: that one "yes" that changes everything.

I wasn't just trying to build anymore.

I was trying to keep something from collapsing.

In Bhubaneswar, I had lost something personal.

In Hyderabad, I was fighting not to lose everything else.

And that's how I lived for the next few weeks —

Split between two cities, two teams, and two versions of myself.

No, Thank You

A week into Hyderabad, I got a reply from one of the VCs I had pitched.

The subject line blinked back at me:

"Re: Pitch – Spatial Intelligence Search for Tangible Item Retrieval"

I had poured my heart into that pitch.

A search engine for real-world items — no GPS, no tagging. Just place or throw your stuff anywhere within a covered space — a house, a mall — and our system would find it. That was the vision. Smart spatial memory. Ambient intelligence.

It was bold.

It was ahead of its time.

It was... mine.

And still — the email read:

Hi Mrinal,

Thanks for reaching out and sharing your product vision.

While we appreciate the creativity behind your approach, this doesn't currently align with our thematic investment thesis.

We wish you all the best in building your solution.

Warm regards,

Blue Blood Capital Venture

Just like that.

A no, dressed in polite corporatespeak.

I stared at it. For too long.

Then closed the laptop.

Not slammed.

Not punched.

Just... closed it like one shuts a door that never opened.

Maybe they didn't get it.

Maybe they weren't ready for a product that searched rooms like Google searched pages.

Or maybe... maybe I was just asking too many people to find things —

when I myself didn't know where I was anymore.

CHAPTER FORTY-FOUR

ROUTINE CALLS AND RUPTURES

Back in my hometown, as per ritual, my wife returned to her parents' house just four days after I left the city.

From Hyderabad, I started calling her every night — not out of affection, but out of duty. It became a routine, like brushing teeth or checking email. One call. Every night. Just enough to tick the box.

She usually spoke about her day, her parents, her relatives — endless stories about cousins and neighbors and hometown gossip.
I listened.

Mostly silent.
Not because I didn't have things to say — but because she didn't care to ask. She wasn't interested in me — just her version of this marriage, whatever that meant to her.

Then one night — about a month in — her voice changed.
Sharper. Controlled.
"Papa said we should ask for ten lakhs... and get the divorce done."
Just like that.
Like it was a business deal.
Like I was a failed investment she wanted to exit with a payout.
For a few seconds, I didn't say anything.
Not out of shock — but because I'd stopped expecting this marriage to mean anything more than a formal sentence.

Ten lakhs.
It wasn't just a number.
It was the cost they'd calculated for my absence, my silence, my emotional vacancy.

And maybe they were right.
Maybe I was too broken to be a husband anymore.
　　But still... this?
　　This felt less like divorce.
More like blackmail.
　　I ended the call that night with a "we'll talk later."
　　But I knew I wouldn't forget that sentence.

CHAPTER FORTY-FIVE

AND THEN SHE REAPPEARED

It had been two months since I last heard anything from her.

Two months have passed since I moved cities.

Two months since I stopped checking her last seen.

Two months of nothing.

And then, out of nowhere — a message.

Soumya:

"I've taken admission in a local engineering college. Applied Electronics and Instrumentation."

That was it.

No hello. No how are you. Just a declaration — like an update she owed to someone who was no longer entitled to anything.

But still...

My fingers moved before my brain could stop them.

"Can we talk? Just for a few minutes?"

She replied after a pause. Not long. Just long enough to feel distant.

Soumya:

"Heading into the library. Will talk later."

That "later" never came.

No follow-up message.

No missed call.

No ping. No voice.

Just silence.

Again.

And I didn't follow up either.

Not because I didn't want to.

But because I finally understood the pattern.

She came when she needed to say something.

Left when I needed her to listen.

That night, I stared at the single line of chat.

Her stream. Her college. Her new life.

And I realized I wasn't part of the update.

I was just one of the people she notified out of habit — like an old contact she hadn't deleted yet.

A week after that message from Soumya — the one that said "Will talk later" and never followed up — I got an email.

It was from one of the VCs I'd pitched.

The subject read:

"Re: Intelligent Item Locator – Proposal Review"

For a second, my heart paused.

I had written to them weeks ago — pitching the product that still felt like the one thing I hadn't failed at.

A search engine for the physical world — no GPS, no trackers.

Place something anywhere — in your room, your house, a mall — and our system would find it. That was the promise. Precision without hardware. Context without satellites.

I clicked the email.

Hi Mrinal,

Thanks for sharing your proposal and vision with us. We found the idea intriguing.

However, it does not align with our current investment direction or verticals of focus.

We wish you all the best in building your solution.

Regards,

Star Investment

That was it.

No feedback. No questions. No second glance.

Just a polite brush-off dressed in venture capital vocabulary.

I read it again — not to understand it better, but because a part of me didn't want to believe that this too was a no.

But it was.

Another no.

I sat there for a while, watching the screen.
Didn't close the laptop.
Didn't curse.
Just... stared.
Outside, the city was noisy again.
Hyderabad never stayed still for long.
But inside me, something had stopped moving.

———————————————————

After shifting to Hyderabad, something finally changed.
No, Soumya didn't message.
The marriage wasn't fixed.
The VCs hadn't said yes.
But my focus returned.
For the first time in months, I started working with real intensity — not just mechanically, but with intention. Because now survival wasn't optional. And maybe that's what I needed — not inspiration, but a deadline.
I poured myself into our projects.
To one of our Dubai clients, I proposed a set of enhancements to the software we'd delivered — features that weren't in the original scope, but would make their systems faster, more intuitive, more powerful.
They loved the suggestions.
Approved them.
Agreed to pay more for the added work.
It wasn't a windfall.
But it was hope.
And in my current world, hope was currency.
The work kept coming.
And I kept delivering.
And somewhere in the flow of proposals, commits, invoices, and team calls... something beautiful happened.
One day — just one day — I woke up, worked, ate, worked again... and never thought of her.
Not once.
Not in the shower.
Not during a break.
Not while closing my eyes at night.

And when I realized that...
I smiled.
A small, private smile.
Not of arrogance. But of quiet triumph.
For months, she had lived in every pause.
And now, finally, I had paused... without her voice filling the silence.
Yes. I am winning.

<u>**One Day Later**</u>
March 10,2015 at 1:03 AM.
Just a day after my quiet victory — after I had gone an entire 24 hours without thinking of her — she called.
Her name flashed on the screen like it had never left.
For a few seconds, I didn't move.
Just stared.
Because I knew — this wasn't casual.
She never called me casually anymore.
I picked up.
Her voice was low. Soft. A little shaky.
"I'm on a train to New Delhi... for an Art of Living camp."
A pause.
"I'm in the AC coach. Parents are a few berths away. But something smells... I think someone's drunk. I'm scared."
And then — almost like a child curling into a pillow —
"Will you talk to me? Until I fall asleep? Please..."
I swallowed.
I had no idea what to say.
Because just yesterday, I had convinced myself that I was healing. That I had finally won.
But here she was.
Breaking through that calm like she always did — softly, unintentionally, but completely.
So I did what I always did.
I talked to her.
About nothing. About everything.
About some bug in the Dubai module, about the taste of Hyderabad tea, about how quiet the city felt at night.

She didn't say much.

Just murmured things. Half-sentences.

I could hear the occasional train announcements. The soft hum of the fan above her berth. Her breath, slowly settling.

Eventually, her voice faded into sleep.

Still on call.

Still in a train.

Still pulling me back — just when I thought I'd gotten away.

Funny how one call can undo a whole day of healing.

But maybe that's what loving her meant — healing in circles, not straight lines.

WHAT ARE WE NOW?

The next morning, there was no message.

No "Thanks for last night."

No "I slept well."

Not even a "Sorry for disturbing."

Nothing.

The call had ended sometime after she drifted into sleep. I stayed on for a while — just listening to the rhythm of the train, her breath, the quiet.

And now it was morning again.

Just like before.

Except something had shifted — not in her, but in me.

For the first time, I wasn't hurt.

I was... curious.

What are we now?

Was I still someone she trusted — or just someone convenient to call at 1 AM when no one else picked up?

Was I a person in her life — or just a leftover echo from her past?

She didn't call to ask how I was.

She didn't call to say she missed me.

She called because she was scared.

And when the fear passed — so did I.

But then I asked myself something harder:

Why can't I call her when I'm the one breaking?

Why do I wait and wait... and say nothing?

Is it ego?

Or is it fear — the fear of being treated like I don't matter anymore?

I knew the answer, but I hated admitting it.

Because I wasn't silent out of pride.
I was silent out of fragility.
I didn't want to hear her cold voice.
Or worse, her disinterest.
I didn't want to be reminded that the person I still missed could live just fine without knowing how I was doing.
So I said nothing.
I always said nothing.
And maybe that's what made her calls so unfair.
She got to reach out whenever she needed me.
But I... I could never bring myself to do the same.
I wasn't her emergency.
I was just her emergency contact.
And maybe I let it happen.
Maybe I still would.
But this time... I didn't feel like her call meant what it used to.
This time, I felt like I was waking up.

November 15, 2017- 3:05AM
I deleted her number today.
No grand gesture, no dramatic pause. Just a few taps on a screen... and years of chaos, comfort, and unanswered questions vanished into digital dust.
Then came the tears. Not loud or furious—just quiet, aching rivers.
As if my heart was saying goodbye to something it never fully had,
but never stopped holding onto.
It hurt. God, it hurt.
But strangely... it also felt like unclenching a fist I didn't know I'd kept closed for so long.
There's a silence now.
Not empty—but sacred.
A silence that holds the echo of her laugh, the weight of her words, the warmth of what could have been.
And still, it whispers back:
It's time.
Maybe healing doesn't always roar.
Sometimes, it just sighs—after finally letting go.

CHAPTER FORTY-SEVEN

OBEDIENCE AND OTHER BETRAYALS

A few weeks after the silence, I had to return home.

There was a ritual — part of post-marriage customs — where the husband brings his wife back from her parents' house. I didn't feel anything. Not excitement. Not hesitation. Just quiet compliance — something I had grown used to.

I stayed two days at her parents' place.

The house was busy with relatives, sweets, polite questions. But one afternoon, her father pulled me aside. What he said next would stay with me far longer than anything else in that house.

"My daughter studied only till Class 5."

I looked at him, confused.

"We didn't think girls need to study beyond basic reading and writing. More education spoils them."

And then — with an almost casual smile:

"When I told your father that, he said — 'My son is very obedient. He'll marry wherever I tell him to.'"

I felt the floor fall away from under me.

My father — the man I had trusted with every major decision in life — had reduced me to a bargaining chip. He never told me she had discontinued her education. Never told me about their beliefs. Never even paused to ask what I wanted.

He hadn't arranged a marriage.
He had arranged a compromise, and used my loyalty to seal it.

I brought her back the next day.

There was no conversation between us.
No closeness. No hope. Just logistics.

I stayed one day at home and returned to Hyderabad.

A week later, she left.

She took her belongings, her jewellery, and even the gold my sister had gifted her — gifts passed with love, not just custom.

She didn't say a word.
Just walked out.

And then... the drama began.

Allegations. Accusations.

"He beats her."
"His family tortured her for dowry."
"She was emotionally and physically abused."
"They threw her out."
"We want a divorce. And   ₹10 lakh as settlement."

They threatened to file a 498A case — the section of IPC meant to protect women from dowry harassment. A law created with good intent, now sharpened into a weapon when truth becomes irrelevant.

I knew I hadn't done anything wrong.
So did my family.

But it didn't matter.

Because in this country, a single accusation under 498A can turn you into a criminal overnight — no trial, no proof, just labels.

Suddenly, I wasn't a son, or a startup founder, or a boy who once loved too hard.

I was a man accused.
A man cornered.

By his own silence.
By his own obedience.
By the misuse of a law designed to protect — now twisted to extort.

They didn't just leave the marriage.
They set fire to it and tried to claim the ashes.

CHAPTER FORTY-EIGHT

EVIDENCE AND EXIT WOUNDS

A few days after the accusations, my father called me.

His voice was tense — the kind that doesn't panic, but has stopped pretending everything's fine.

"We need to act fast," he said.

"They've threatened to file a 498A case. You need to gather proof — dates, evidence — anything that shows you weren't even home during the time they've accused us of harassment."

Fortunately, I wasn't home on those dates.

I had been in Hyderabad the entire time. And I had emails, work records, call logs, even bus tickets to prove it.

My father also told me they were applying for anticipatory bail — just in case. Because under IPC 498A, there was a very real chance that entire families can be arrested first, and asked questions later.

That wasn't fear.

That was legal reality.

There were now so many legal procedures to follow — affidavits, lawyer meetings, bail arguments, police statements.

Thankfully, our neighbors stood by us.

They knew how she was treated — with care, dignity, even affection — despite the emotional distance in the marriage. Some had even seen her laughing with my mother, casually chatting in the verandah.

We also had multiple photos and home videos.

Moments of her smiling, enjoying festivals, eating with the family.

Even recordings from days when I wasn't home — visual proof that there was no tension, no threat, no mistreatment.

The case dragged for a few months.
Multiple hearings. Legal back and forth.

And then, the shift happened.

Her family realized they were not going to win if the case moved forward. The facts didn't support their story. The witnesses weren't on their side. The court wasn't blind.

They approached us with an offer: out-of-court settlement.

They had started with ₹10 lakh — like it was some kind of compensation for a play they wrote and performed.

But eventually, they had to settle for 50% of it.

I later found out this wasn't the first time her father had done something like this. He had pulled a similar stunt with another daughter's marriage — extorting money through staged legal drama.

My father had never checked.
Never asked questions.
Never investigated the background.

He just... trusted.
Just like I had trusted him.

By the middle of 2018, the case was closed.
The drama ended.
The papers were signed.
And for the first time in a long time...
I could breathe.

Not because justice was perfect.
But because truth — slowly, painfully — had done its job.

CHAPTER FORTY-NINE

WHAT REMAINED AFTER THE FIRE

When the case finally closed, life didn't jump back to normal.

It walked.

One slow, tired step at a time.

And somewhere in that quiet aftermath, I came closer to my family again.

Not because I forgot what had happened...

But because I had finally accepted it.

I had also grown a new habit —

I no longer trusted my father blindly.

I had learned to take my own decisions.

To pause.

To ask.

To doubt — even the people I loved.

But some things... still hurt in ways I couldn't explain.

I wanted to share everything — the court case, the betrayal, the relief — with Soumya.

But only if she wanted to listen.

She didn't.

She had become a stranger.

And I had grown tired of expecting even a "hi" that never came.

So I finally did it.

Deleted our WhatsApp chat.

Deleted every message on Facebook Messenger.

Unfriended her.

But...

I couldn't delete the photos.

The ones she had once sent me — casually, playfully, without knowing they'd one day become relics.

And I couldn't delete her voice notes.

Sometimes, late at night, I'd play them like songs —

not to relive,

but to feel something familiar.

Her laughter. Her pauses. Her sleepy "goodnight"s.

They became part of my playlist.

My lullabies.

The only music I couldn't replace.

Almost four years passed.

I moved cities.

Worked on myself.

Moved on — or so I told people.

But inside...

I still searched for reasons to hate her.

I wanted to.

I needed to.

Because anger is easier to carry than longing.

But I failed.

Every single time.

Because no matter how much I tried,

my heart refused to accept that she was selfish.

Not even for a second.

CHAPTER FIFTY

THE LAST ASK

It was October 2020 — deep into the quiet months of COVID.

Most people were reconnecting with old friends, sending "Are you okay?" messages across forgotten chat windows.

I wasn't expecting anything.

Not anymore.

And yet... one message found me.

Facebook Messenger. From Soumya.

"If you're free and comfortable, can you share your number? Or you can call me on this one."

She had sent it two days earlier.

I saw it late — on the 20th of October.

My heart didn't race. It didn't ache.

It just... paused.

I replied. Gave her my number.

Not because I was excited.

But because a part of me still wanted to believe she remembered me beyond her reasons.

That night — or rather early morning, around 2:00 AM — she called.

Her voice hadn't changed.

Neither had her rhythm — casual, bright, confident.

She spoke for almost an hour.

About college.

About dreams after graduation.

About how engineering was over, and how the world looked now.

And then... she got to the point.

"Actually, I called because one of my friends needs some technical help. I thought maybe you could guide..."

And just like that, my chest went quiet again.
She hadn't called to ask if I was okay.
Not to say *"I thought of you."*
Not even to ask "How have you been?"
She had called for something.
Again.
And suddenly, I didn't feel tired.
I felt empty.
I told her I didn't have that kind of time anymore.
She paused.
Didn't argue.
Didn't explain.
Just hung up.
That was the last time we spoke.
I deleted her number again.
Deleted the message thread from Messenger — the same place it had all restarted.
This time, there was no grief.
No playlist.
No night walk with her voice in my ear.
Just silence.
And finally...
acceptance.

CHAPTER FIFTY-ONE

THE OFFER

November 14, 2020

The day was like any other.

Meetings. Deadlines. Coffee gone cold.

And then the email arrived.

Subject: Collaboration Proposal – Apple Inc.

I blinked.

Read it again.

And again.

They had found our paper. Our prototype. That crazy little thing we built to help people find items in malls and homes — something born out of frustration, hustle, and too many sleepless nights.

They said it resembled an internal concept they were working on.

They called it Apple Tag.

And they wanted us.

The proposal came straight from Cupertino:

"We would like to acquire your patent and core technology. Our offer: $30 million."

Thirty.

Million.

Dollars.

Hitesh froze when I read it out loud. Dhiraj dropped his phone.

We stared at each other in disbelief.

Tears welled up.

Not from greed.

But from validation.

From an idea that once lived in a 300 sq ft rented room with three second-hand laptops and a head full of madness.

It was happening.
The world had finally noticed.
I wanted to message Soumya.
Just to say — "Look... we did it."
But I didn't.
She was no longer there.
Not in the inbox. Not in the moments.
Only in memory.
And so, we signed the deal.
With trembling hands and silent hearts.
The world called it a business acquisition.
But to me,
It was closure.

CHAPTER FIFTY-TWO

THE LETTER I NEVER SENT

Dear Soumya,

I'm not writing this for you to read.
I'm writing this because I need to breathe.
There was a time when your messages felt like oxygen.
A simple "hi" from you could fix a terrible day.
And your silence... could ruin a peaceful one.
And then came the years.
The years where you vanished.
Then came back.
Then vanished again.
The years where I stayed —
Available.
Even when I was broken,
Even when I was accused of things I hadn't done,
Even when I was quietly crying behind glowing startup dashboards,
fighting court cases in the day and loneliness by night.
You called when you were afraid.
You called when you were alone.
You called when you needed something.
But not once — not once — did you ever call just to ask,
"How are you?"
Even when my life was falling apart.
Even when I was being dragged into false allegations.
Even when I was silently choosing to survive...

You didn't ask.
And I didn't tell.
Maybe I was scared.
Scared of your indifference.
Scared that you no longer saw me — not as a contact, but as the person who stood by you when no one else did.
I tried to hate you.
God knows, I tried.
But my heart never agreed.
Because even now, when I hear your voice in old recordings,
I don't feel anger.
I feel a strange warmth — like holding a burnt letter that still carries the scent of a better time.
Soumya,
You weren't cruel.
You weren't evil.
You were just... not mine.
And that truth took me years to accept.
Now I'm scared.
Too scared.
Scared to even message you.
Scared of the silence that might follow.
Scared of the wrong reply to a silly joke.
I had built a bad habit — of sharing everything with you.
And fortunately, slowly, I broke it.
I kept asking myself —
Why am I scared of you?
Why?
Maybe this wasn't love.
Maybe this was Pagalpanthy.
But if I'm born again, I'd still choose this madness over a thousand peaceful lives.
But now...
This is my goodbye.
Not with pain.
Not with regret.
But with peace.

Just one request —
Please don't call me again.
Please don't message me.
    It takes years to forget you —
And every ping from you is like tearing open a healed wound.
    You were a chapter I kept rereading.
But now,
I've finally put the book down.
And I'm walking into a life that no longer waits for your reply.
    Take care,
The man who once kept your voice in his playlist.

CHAPTER FIFTY-THREE

EPILOGUE: PLATFORM NUMBER ONE

December 22, 2024, Chennai Central Railway Station.

I wasn't supposed to be there.

My flight had been rescheduled. The client meeting got pushed too.
I had a few hours to kill, and my hotel was walking distance from Chennai Central.

So I drifted into the station — just out of habit... or maybe memory.

Trains hissed. People moved with urgency. Platform announcements echoed like old stories.

And then I saw her...

Soumya.

Slightly older now. A woman, not a girl.
Wearing a simple cotton saree, hair loosely tied, face half-lit by the yellow platform lights.

And next to her... a boy.
Maybe two or three years old.

He was tugging at her hand, pointing to a packet of biscuits in a vendor's basket.

"Mrinal want that!"

I froze.

Mrinal.

My name.

He said it twice — clumsily, like children do when they've only just begun to own language.

Soumya didn't correct him.

She didn't say, "That's not your name."
She didn't say, "Say it properly."
She smiled.
And said softly, like a lullaby:
"Okay, Mrinal beta... one only."
And just like that, she had named her world — after mine.
I didn't move.
I didn't call out.
I just stood there, watching from behind a pillar, heart silent, breath held like a broken promise.
She didn't see me.
Or maybe... she did.
Maybe she always would.
The train arrived.
She picked up the child, adjusted his bag, and stepped in.
For a moment, as she leaned by the window, she looked out.
Our eyes met — not for long.
Just enough to say everything without saying anything.
And then the train pulled away.
No goodbye.
No explanation.
Just a boy named Mrinal...
and a past that had named him.

Some stories never end.
They just leave you standing on a platform — wondering if you were real, or just remembered.

About The Author

Mrityunjay Kumar is a software entrepreneur by profession and a storyteller by heart. With a background in engineering and years of experience building tech startups, he never imagined that one day he'd find himself pouring his emotions into pages rather than code.

His debut novel, Pagalpanthy, is not just a work of fiction—it's a soul echo. Inspired by a story shared in quiet trust nearly a decade ago, it weaves through the turbulence of unspoken love, the ache of emotional disarray, and the fragile beauty of youth slipping by. What started as restless scribbles under dim light became a journey not of invention, but of remembrance—of feeling someone else's truth so deeply, it demanded to be retold.

Beyond his entrepreneurial success, Mrityunjay has always been drawn toward human emotion, memory, and the quiet resilience of the heart. His writing is deeply personal, often blurring the line between fiction and reality.

When he's not juggling business calls or tech sprints, he enjoys reading books , learning new tech, or revisiting old conversations that once changed everything.

He believes that some stories are not written—they are relived, word by word.

Email ID: mrityunjaytech@gmail.com
facebook : @mrityunjaykumarmishra
Like us : https://www.facebook.com/pagalpanthyBegins/